Partisan Wedding

Partisan Wedding

Stories by
Renata Viganò

Translated with an Introduction
by
Suzanne Branciforte

University of Missouri Press
Columbia and London

Library of Congress Cataloging–in–Publication Data

Viganò, Renata, 1900–1976.
  [Matrimonio in brigata. English]
  Partisan wedding : stories / by Renata Viganò ; translated
with an introduction by Suzanne Branciforte.
      p.   cm.
  Includes biblographical references.
  ISBN 0-8262-1228-X (pa. : alk. paper)
  1. World War, 1939–1945—Underground movements—
Italy—Fiction.
I. Branciforte, Suzanne. II. Title.
PQ4882.I27M313 1999
853' .914—dc21   99–37940
                                                                              CIP

♾ This paper meets the requirements of the
American National Standard for Permanence of Paper
for Printed Library Materials, Z39.48, 1984.

Text designer: Liz Young
Cover designer: Mindy Shouse
Typesetter: Crane Composition
Printer and binder: Edwards Brothers, Inc.
Typefaces: New Baskerville

To the women of courage that I have known, whose battles were not fought in wartime, but who wouldn't give in or give up, and who by their example showed me how: Audrey, Carmel, Carola, Kathy, Liana, Marcella, Regina, and Mamma Terri. And to Kristi and Gina, students of the resistance, for their encouragement and support.

For Max, as always.

Contents

Partisan Wedding

Introduction

by Suzanne Branciforte

Renata Viganò: Life and Works

Renata Viganò was born June 17, 1900, in Bologna.
Her early childhood was marked by good fortune and
relative wealth. Her bourgeois family upbringing was
due in part to the efforts of her maternal great-grandmother, who started a famous company that produced
and rented luxury coaches for weddings, baptisms, and
funerals. The image of her strong, independent female
ancestor clearly had an impact on Viganò. Even her inclination to write may be traced to the influence of this
great-grandmother, Caterina Mazzetti, who herself composed "strange moralistic poetry."[1] However, Viganò's
idyllic childhood came to an abrupt end when her family's fortunes declined and the family business failed. In
her later writings she recognizes her privileged background and discusses her bourgeois origins in light of
her later participation in the Resistance and subse-
quent involvement in Italy's Communist Party. Viganò's
schooling was incomplete: she attended a classical high
school for three years after a brief try at a technical institute. As she later admits in "My Resistance," she
would have liked to have pursued a career in medicine
as a doctor, but did not attend a university. Her mother

1. Enzo Colombo, "Le opere e i giorni," 99.

died in 1926, her father in 1928; thus, Viganò was forced to work to earn a living. She became a nurse and, as she later states, earned her place "in the working class" ("My Resistance").

Viganò's lifelong dedication to writing began at an early age; she published two books of poetry written in adolescence, *Ginestra in fiore* (1913) and *Piccola fiamma* (1916). When the first collection appeared, it created a stir in the local literary world, due to Viganò's age. The famous Italian author Ada Negri wrote to the young poet, who was considered a child prodigy.[2] After this brief and intense debut, Viganò almost completely ceased her literary activity. Only the romantic novel *Il lume spento,* which came out in 1933 and was dedicated to her mother's memory, spanned this period of silence.[3] She began to write again only at the conclusion of the war, after her experience as a nurse, *staffetta* (courier), and partisan.

Viganò's best-known work is the neorealist novel *L'Agnese va a morire* (1949), which won the esteemed Italian literary award the Viareggio prize and was adapted to the cinema by the director Giuliano Montaldo in 1976.[4] Despite the positive reception of the novel and its later adaptation to film, little critical attention has

2. Ibid., 107.
3. Ibid., 114.
4. I have pointed out elsewhere how Viganò, while representative of a generation of writers who dedicated their lives and voices to recounting World War II, has a unique and distinctively female voice. See my essay "In a Different Voice: Women Writing World War II."

been paid Renata Viganò's work, a fact lamented by Italian critics. Indeed, Viganò's entire body of work has been completely inaccessible to an English-speaking audience until now.[5] In addition to her most famous work, Viganò published two collections of short stories: *Arriva la cicogna* (1954), and *Matrimonio in brigata,* here translated as *Partisan Wedding,* published in 1976, the year of her death. Two other novels appeared in the postwar period, *Ho conosciuto Ciro* (1959), and *Una storia di ragazze* (1962). *Donne nella Resistenza* (1955) is a useful reference volume; it is a compendium of brief biographies of women who gave their lives to the Resistance. The Italian National Association of Partisans (ANPI) published posthumously a collection of later poetry, *Rosario* (1984).

Viganò's journalistic activity was widespread: the newspapers and journals to which she contributed include *L'Unità, Noi donne, Rinascita, Il Ponte, Il Progresso d'Italia,* and *Il Corriere padano.* In 1955, a rupture with the PCI (the Italian Communist Party) caused Viganò to briefly interrupt her collaboration with the party's highly regarded newspaper, *L'Unità* and the Italian Communist women's journal, *Noi donne.*

Renata Viganò met her husband, Antonio Meluschi, who was ten years her junior, in 1935. Meluschi, himself a writer and anti-Fascist, introduced Viganò to Communism, and he became her political mentor as well as

5. While Viganò's masterpiece *L'Agnese va a morire* has been translated into fourteen languages, it has never found its way into English. See my article "In a Different Voice."

her closest reader and critic. Meluschi had been in prison in Rome, where he met Antonio Gramsci, a key figure in the formation of the Italian Communist Party and founder of the paper *L'Unità.* Gramsci called Meluschi *"lo struzzo"* (the ostrich). Viganò and Meluschi were married in September 1937; they later adopted a son, Agostino, whom they affectionately called "Bu."

Viganò's involvement in the Italian Resistance is well documented and is the principal subject matter of her fiction. Her battle name was *Contessa,* referring to her upper-class background. The entire family was involved in the partisan war: Antonio Meluschi was the commander of a partisan brigade, and Viganò acted as a *staffetta,* a nurse, and even an official. They took their son Agostino with them into hiding in the lowlands of Emilia-Romagna where they fought.

In the postwar period, the Viganò-Meluschi home on Via Mascarella in Bologna was a famous cultural and political meeting place where many writers, thinkers, Communists, and former partisans continued to gather until Renata Viganò's death, in April 1976.

The Partisan War

In many ways the Resistance—the clandestine opposition to Fascism—in Italy represents the moment of greatest cooperation and purest collaboration among those who opposed Mussolini and his regime. The partisan war brought together people from all social strata and it broke across regional boundaries as people united in the fight against Fascism. Hierarchical divisions were blurred: divisions of class and gender, political orientation, and educational background mattered little in the Resistance. Partisans working shoulder to shoulder came from the entire political spectrum, from Communists to Catholics. And the importance of women in the functioning of the partisan war in Italy cannot be underestimated: while they may not have fired guns themselves (although sometimes they did even that), they did transport munitions, carry food to detachments in remote places, cook and clean for the rebel soldiers, relay messages, take in and care for the wounded, among other things.

The resistance to Fascism began with Fascism itself, in the 1920s. Opponents to Mussolini's regime, like Carlo Levi (author of *Christ Stopped at Eboli*) were imprisoned or sent into domestic exile *(confino)* in the south of Italy. Two of the primary political forces in the formation of an organized Resistance were the Italian Communist Party and the Action Party *(Partito d'Azione)*.

The tumultuous events of the summer of 1943 witnessed extraordinary change in Italy's position in the Second World War and created a climate of confusion. Italy had entered the war on the side of Germany, as one of the Axis powers, when Mussolini signed an agreement with Hitler, the Pact of Steel, in 1939. Shortly after the Allies invaded Sicily in July 1943, Mussolini fell from power. What followed was a chaotic attempt at order that left three forms of government in Italy: Mussolini's reconstituted government, known as the Republic of Salò; the Kingdom of the South, ruled by the Italian king and his appointed prime minister, Marshal Badoglio; and the CLNAI, the Committee for the National Liberation of Upper Italy, the leading partisan organ located in Milan.

By September 1943, Badoglio managed to orchestrate an armistice with the Allies that was officially declared on September 8. At that moment, Italy ceased to be a part of the Axis powers; and while never officially joining the Allied cause, Italy declared a "co-belligerent" status against the Axis. Thus began the period of German occupation in central and northern Italy, and the enormous Allied push for liberation. As Carlo D'Este has pointed out, the Italian campaign was the "longest, dreariest and most expensive Allied endeavor of the entire war."[6] Since the liberation began in the south and moved slowly up the peninsula over the course of the next two years, the Resistance war was fought for a longer period in the north, particularly in the regions of Piemonte, Liguria, Lombardia, Emilia-Romagna, and the Veneto.

Renata Viganò's focus on women's participation in the Resistance filters the female experience of the war in Italy into fictional narrative. Women served in the partisan war in many ways, although often their participation has been overlooked. One of the most common positions for women partisans was as a *staffetta*. Such go-betweens were essential to the functioning of clandestine activity. In effect, women relied on their female

6. Carlo D'Este, *Bitter Victory: The Battle for Sicily, 1943*, 552.

identity in order to surreptitiously convey arms, food, messages, and other things to their male colleagues. It is ironic but no accident that the invaluable service performed by thousands of women *staffette* depended on their femaleness, thus "exploiting the male habit of ascribing specific roles to women."[7]

Anna Maria Bruzzone and Rachele Farina describe the many tasks accorded women partisans in their work *La Resistenza taciuta (The Silenced Resistance)*:

> . . . the partisan struggle saw women in the GAPs and SAPs [resistance groups], in the formations in the plains and in the mountains, in the distribution of clandestine newspapers and information, in extremely dangerous liaison missions. Not only as "mothers" of the partisans or cooks or nurses of hungry or wounded rebels, even if they were also this, and when all this could signify arrest, burning of your house, execution. Women were the most solid, firm links in the network, often risking more than the men because, if captured, the enemy reserved for women carnal violence that never touched the men.[8]

One of the major revelations of Bruzzone and Farina's work is that the officially reported statistics reflecting female participation in the Resistance effort at war's end were surely erroneous, and underestimate the number

7. Anna Maria Bruzzone, "Women in the Italian Resistance," 279.
8. Anna Maria Bruzzone and Rachele Farina, *La Resistenza taciuta,* 11 (translation mine).

of women *partigiane* who actively and routinely performed duties to keep the Resistance movement going.

Anna Bravo distinguishes "participation in" from
"being part of" the war effort. More than just a semantic
argument, Bravo is concerned with how history has
viewed women and war:

> . . . while the texts about the Resistance are classified
> under "Participation in . . . ," a formula that presents
> women like occasional guests in a history not their own,
> where normality and the norm are the actions of men:
> to *participate in* does not equal *to be a part of*. . .9

More attention was given women's participation in the
war after the advent of feminist scholarship, beginning
in the late seventies and eighties.[10] Bravo credits a shift in
methodological approach and historiographic traditions
for the newfound interest in women's roles in the war.
She finds that "the phase of the legitimation of the
Resistance as a historiographic object and of its inclusion
as a founding myth of the national and state identity"[11]

9. Anna Bravo, introduction to *Donne e uomini nelle guerre
mondiali*, v (translation and emphasis mine).

10. However, more scholarly attention has been paid to
women under Fascism; Mussolini's programs to keep women in
the home and out of the workplace, bearing children who in
turn subscribed to Fascist propaganda in the schools, has been
well documented. See Victoria De Grazia's *How Fascism Ruled
Women: Italy, 1922-1945*, and Tracy Koon's *Believe, Obey, Fight:
Political Socialization of Youth in Fascist Italy, 1922-1943*.

11. Bravo, introduction to *Donne e uomini*, vi.

leads to the unearthing of women's vital roles in the creation of the Italian state. Thus, the importance of the myth of the Resistance as a political tool fueled the fire for increased scholarship.

The Collection *Partisan Wedding*

Partisan Wedding consists of nineteen stories: seventeen fictional short stories and two autobiographical accounts ("Acquitted" and "My Resistance"). According to Andrea Battistini, "the entire book . . . retraces all the canonical stations of partisan life."[12]

Clearly, all of Viganò's stories are more or less autobiographical, based on her real-life participation; we even come to identify certain characters who repeat or certain incidents that may be referred to in more than one story. Thus, it becomes possible to piece together bits of history and, in turn, to truly appreciate the rhetorical skill of the author in her fictional renderings of painful memories. In the personal essays, we get a glimpse at what Viganò's own actions were during the war. As a result, we are able to appreciate how she thought about the events she experienced and translated them into narrative. She gives so much of her source material in the autobiographical essay "My Resistance" that we are able to identify models for characters in other stories. For instance, there is a reference to a partisan named Fabio who is killed on the day of

12. Andrea Battistini, "Due esistenze avventurose," 48 (translation mine).

liberation, and who clearly served as the model for Nigrein's brother in the story "Trap Shoot."

Through Viganò's stories, one comes to know the geography of Emilia-Romagna, her home province. Through repeated description of the landscape, it becomes vivid, familiar. We can envision the plains—the threatening, naked plains—and the transparent, disclosing water and appreciate how hard it must have been to fight a clandestine war in that naked expanse.[13] Viganò's vision is limited to that region, her home, where she and her husband fought the war. In this respect, her narrative bears out Italo Calvino's description of the Resistance: "My landscape was something jealously mine. . . . I had a landscape. . . . The Resistance represented the fusion of landscape with people."[14]

Indeed, Viganò's work exemplifies the neorealist style, a movement in literature and film that grew out of the war experience in Italy. Viganò uses the limited palette of a neorealist film: black, white, and infinite shades of gray. There is an emphasis on light, on landscape, and on the struggle common to the people of the area she is describing. Not accidentally, these colors —black, white, and gray, or what could be seen as the implicit lack of color—reflect the struggle between

13. The final segment of Rossellini's monumental war epic, *Paisà*, transfers to film the light and transparency of that region.

14. Calvino's important discussion of neorealism is contained in the 1964 preface to his novel *The Path to the The Nest of Spiders*, viii–ix.

good and evil and the many moral ambiguities faced by those involved in the war. The lack of color reflects a dim limbo and an ongoing conflict in time of war. Another characteristic of neorealism that Viganò employs is the actual language of the direct participants. Often Viganò's characters speak in dialect, but unlike filmic versions of stories of war and the Resistance, the dialogues are actually written in Italian. Thus no barrier is created between author and reader; rather, there is merely the indication in the narration that a particular line was spoken in the regional language. Finally, Viganò focuses on unheroic characters, simple, real people whose lives were shattered by the events of the war.

Stylistically, Viganò prefers long sentences, which have been truncated at times for the conventions of English. Her prose is imagistic and poetic and underscores her inclination toward poetry. Viganò explains her wartime duties in frank, detailed language using an economy of expression. Her prose is sprinkled with incomplete sentences that somehow punctuate what she is saying and give rhythm to the otherwise long flow of words. The incomplete sentences tend to rapidly sketch details, like a quick brush stroke, adding some aspect to our perception of the whole. Her language is sensual, involving all the senses in her descriptions. Viganò does not shrink from what is hard, ugly, and real; hers is a real neorealism. In "My Resistance," in an image akin to a brutal photojournalism of the war, she states: "We saw dead children with their little faces still shining from tears and life. It seemed impossible that they would

never again get up and run in their broken shoes."
There is a rawness in her descriptions; she does not
avoid the brutal facts but tells us of war's reality simply
and directly. There is no place for fear or modesty in
Viganò's accounts of the war.

The war is the protagonist of Viganò's narrative, not
just a setting or background. The war is a character, a
constant presence. And what emerges from the stories
is the war's profile; in fact, Viganò has organized her
text to vaguely trace a chronology of the war, taking us
beyond April 25, 1945, and the liberation. More than
once she hints at the long wait for the Allies' arrival, and
it is not without a little annoyance that she states how
the Anglo-American forces slowed their advance as a
long, difficult winter dragged on. The difficulty the partisans had maintaining themselves and the guerrilla war
through the winter of 1944 is vividly conveyed in her stories. The Fascists and Germans had to be fought off as
the Italians waited for the Allies, their "liberators."

Viganò goes beyond the limit of dates, which are too
precise and unreal in a conflict that so involved the
world, her country, her province. In the two stories that
take us beyond the actual liberation, she shows how the
tensions clearly extended beyond the end of the war.
The thinly veiled personal reminiscence on her husband's arrest, "Acquitted," hints at the civil war that
plagued Italy in the long months following the April
1945 liberation. As Viganò's first-person narrator describes, animosity between former Fascists and partisans did not cease with the end of the war; killings and

imprisonments continued, and the tensions were played out in repeated retaliations.

At the war's start, Viganò was one of the older partisans, many of whom were little more than children. Born in 1900, she was a mature participant, an adult woman and a mother. This fact is not to be discounted, as it affects her entire perception of the war and life in general. Thematically, she treats how and why people became involved in the partisan struggle, the search for meaning, the moral struggle, and the extreme difficulty in assigning values. She answers the question Italo Calvino posed in his first novel, *The Path to the Nest of Spiders,* regarding the partisans: "What drives them to lead this life, what makes them fight?"[15]

Viganò undeniably focuses on women and their roles, not only profiling the familiar form of the *staffetta,* but the many and varied roles and activities in which women engaged. Viganò is not myopic; her vision includes women who were enemies of the partisans, women who betrayed them. Her perspective on women's roles mirrors the complexities and ambiguities of the men's world; that is to say, she sheds light on female participation without painting a rosy or easy picture. Just as women are capable of acts of heroism, physical force, cleverness, and courage, so too are they capable of betrayal and treason. In stories that focus on conflict, on the struggle between good and evil, Viganò

15. Calvino, *Path to the Nest of Spiders,* 101.

is careful to point out that the contrast between black and white is not so clear-cut, that there are a million shades of gray. Her complex vision reveals the subtleties of human character. Attention to the minutiae of life, and a Carver-like focus on the quiet desperation of ordinary lives set against the backdrop of an important historical moment, characterizes her style as she contrasts the ordinary with the epic.

The women whom Viganò describes in the short stories are mothers, wives, lovers, sisters. They maintain their outstanding ability to nurture and to care, fighting to remain human, to preserve their female qualities in the face of war. Even Viganò's images are often linked to the world of female activity: cloth-based activities like sewing, knitting, and doing laundry, or food-related activities like cooking. Her concentration on the maternal bond is one of the distinguishing characteristics of her narrative. For Viganò, women are nurturing and representative of the potential for life and procreation; thus, in some measure, women represent the antithesis of war, which is life-depriving.

The women of Viganò's stories are inspiring in their simplicity. Many are the women who join the partisan struggle in response to what was done to their husbands ("Red Flag" and "Wool Socks"), fathers ("Argelide"), or brothers ("Campalbo" and "Trap Shoot"). Maternal concerns are preeminent, whether those of a mother who does not want to see her children die for an ideology ("Portrait of Garibaldi"), or those of a son who has joined the partisans and wants his mother warned, so she doesn't wait or worry uselessly ("November 1943").

In the story "Death of a Mother," Viganò focuses on a particular mother-son relationship, while telling of another wartime experience, that of Italian Jews and deportation. This experience has been treated more fully by Giorgio Bassani and Primo Levi, but Viganò's inclusion of it reflects her concern with portraying the full range of wartime experiences. Whether the figure of the mother is the protagonist, or whether she is absent but hovers in the background like a silhouette or a cameo, Viganò privileges the mother-child relationship and carefully profiles the many permutations in her stories.

The title story, "Partisan Wedding," sets the tone for the collection. The simplicity of the characters, the humble wedding set against a backdrop of war, underscores the drama. The ominous quality that pervades the story puts the reader ill at ease, and reminds us of the ever-present threat of danger and of death. The innocence of the young bride, Marina, now involved in helping a partisan brigade, gives an inside look at how some women became involved in the Resistance and how the clandestine war was fought on a personal level. Other women, like the mother fighting a war while her son sleeps ("Peter"), or the thirteen-year-old girl who brings copies of L'Unità to the partisans in her sick brother's stead ("Campalbo"), provide us with examples of awesome courage and humbling determination.

In many stories, sex and sexuality are treated frankly by Viganò ("Red Flag," "Argelide," "Big Opportunity," "Thin Walls," and "Last Action"). Nowhere is Viganò's attention to women's issues and their ability to parlay their femaleness into strategic wartime advantage more evident than in the story "Red Flag." The story's title is a clever play on words, referring both to a symbol of Communism (the red flag) and of what defines and unites women (the red blood of menstruation). Just as the female protagonist, Amedea, does not shrink from utilizing a soiled sanitary pad to cover munitions, Viganò does not shrink from describing menstruation, prostitution, and strategic use of female sexuality, to show how her characters employed their femaleness to achieve a desired end. One of the recurring conditions of women in wartime, prostitution, is treated with an understanding and compassion that is deeply moving ("Argelide" and "Big Opportunity"). In two stories, women are condemned for using their sexuality to betray partisans ("Last Action" and "Thin Walls").

In the final piece of the collection *Partisan Wedding*, Viganò provides valuable insight about her most famous female character, L'Agnese, the heroine of her masterpiece, *L'Agnese va a morire*. In this nonfictional essay, Viganò discusses the genesis of her prototypical female partisan and provides us with important information on how she formed a composite model based on women she knew during the clandestine war. The characteristics Viganò chose to assemble this quintessential *partigiana* tell us much about her style and focus, and bear out Viganò's adherence to the tenets of neorealism. L'Agnese is an antimodel, she is antiheroic. She is not politically committed, her discourse is free of polemics. She is a fat, massive, peasant woman; she is old. She is maternal but ironically and deliberately not a mother. This essay allows us a glimpse into the author's mind and craft: Viganò has filtered life experiences and characteristics of real women she knew and has given us a synthetic archetype.

But it is perhaps the conclusion of the volume, ambiguous for its antiheroic stance, where Viganò reveals herself most. She underscores the deep bond she feels to her region, to the landscape that defines her. In simple, unadorned, poetic language, she remembers the moment of liberation and the inconclusiveness of that experience. There were no "exultant crowds, nor hugs, nor flags in the sun." There is no victory on the day of liberation, there is no easy endpoint as the shots still resound in a land torn by political and ideological conflict. By ending her volume in this way, there is no conclusion to the conflict, and Viganò denies us conclusion as well. In a bittersweet memory that is a powerful antiwar statement, Viganò reminds us of what feminists have long repeated, that "the personal is political," and the political is personal.

Glossary

Battle names. The partisans all took assumed names to protect their true identities. The battle names were usually one word that somehow described the person who adopted it, commonly a characteristic or trait, or a name other than one's own, usually with some significance. Sometimes the terms were foreign, often in English, or in the dialect of the region. Some examples of battle names are Red Wolf, Lefty, Johnny, Annie, Negrein. In this translation, most of the battle names that connote some quality of the person bearing the name have been translated into English to convey that meaning; others, that are simply names, have been left in the original Italian.

Black Brigade. A Fascist militia, composed of "Blackshirts," fighting for the Republic of Salò.

Blackshirts. A way to refer to Italian Fascists, due to their dress code of wearing black shirts. The troops of the Republic of Salò were referred to in this way.

Carabinieri. The Italian state police.

CLN (Comitato per la liberazione nazionale). The Committee for National Liberation, which formed in Rome on September 9, 1943, after the armistice. This group brought together the anti-Fascist parties: the Communists, the Socialists, the Action Party, the

Liberals, and the Christian Democrats. They joined forces to fight against the German occupation. After Mussolini's fall and the king's escape, this group acted as a form of government for Italy.

CLNAI (Comitato per la liberazione dell'Alta Italia). The National Committee for the Liberation of Upper Italy, which was located in Milan. After January 1944, the CLN in Rome designated the group in Milan as a form of government for the north, where it became the most important organ of the Resistance.

Formation. The term denotes the structural organization of the partisans, the smallest unit being a formation or group.

GAP (Gruppi di Azione Patriottica). The first groups of partisans who organized clandestine terrorist acts against Fascists and Germans in the cities. Their members were also called *gappisti* but are more commonly referred to as partisans. *GAP* comes to be synonymous with *partisan brigade,* that is, a designation for a group of Resistance fighters working together. Literally, the term means "Groups of Patriotic Action."

Garibaldino. At the beginning of the partisan war, the first formations of Resistance fighters were from the political left. These Communist formations were called the Garibaldi Brigades, and thus their members were called Garibaldini, after Giuseppe Garibaldi, one of the key figures of the Italian Unification.

National Republican Guard. Along with the Black Brigades, one of the four militias associated with the Fascist Republic of Salò, otherwise known as the

Italian Social Republic, formed in 1943 after the fall
of Mussolini.

Repubblichino. A supporter of the Fascist government at
the Republic of Salò.

Salò, Republic of Salò. Salò, a town on Lake Garda, was
the headquarters of Mussolini's puppet regime after
September 1943. This, one of the three governments
of Italy after September 8, was in the hands of the
Germans during occupation.

SAP (Squadre di Azione Patriottica). Groups of workers
usually located in urban areas who organized clandestine actions in support of the Resistance in their
free time. Literally, the term means "Teams of
Patriotic Action."

September 8. This date, in 1943, marks the turning point
in the war for Italy. It is the day the armistice between
Italy and the Allies was announced. Italy began the
war as a partner in the Axis powers, allied with
Germany. On July 25, 1943, Mussolini's government
fell. The Allies had already begun their invasion in
Sicily and were moving up the peninsula. While Italy
was not allowed to formally join the Allied effort, it
declared a cobelligerent status, agreeing to assist the
Allies in the liberation of Italy from German occupation.

Staffetta. Term used most often to describe female partisans, although not all women who participated in the
Resistance were *staffette.* Translated literally, the term
means dispatcher, courier, or relay runner. In fact,
the usual task of a *staffetta* was to relay goods: food,
arms, documents, and so on from one partisan en-

campment or brigade to another. Women were better able to do this because at the time of the Second World War, women were treated differently from men, often with respect or indifference, and therefore less likely to be stopped or searched. Often the *staffette* hid these items under laundry or in shopping bags.

Bibliography

Battistini, Andrea. "Due esistenze avventurose." In *Matrimonio in brigata: Le opere e i giorni di Renata Viganò e Antonio Meluschi,* ed. Enzo Colombo. Bologna: Grafis Edizioni, 1995.

———. *Pugillaria: Le parole in guerra: Lingua e ideologia dell'*Agnese va a morire. Bologna: Italo Bovolenta Editore, 1982.

Bonaparte, Laura. *Giuliano Montaldo e L'Agnese va a morire.* Milan: Ghisoni Editore, 1976.

Branciforte, Suzanne. "In a Different Voice: Women Writing World War II." In *Studies for Dante: Essays in Honor of Dante Della Terza,* ed. Franco Fido, Rena A. Syska-Lamparska, and Pamela D. Stewart. Florence: Edizioni Cadmo, 1998.

Bravo, Anna. *La repubblica partigiana dell'Alto Monferrato.* Turin: G. Giappichelli Editore, 1964.

Bravo, Anna, ed. *Donne e uomini nelle guerre mondiali.* Bari: Laterza, 1991.

Bravo, Anna, and Daniele Jalla, eds. *La vita offesa: Storia e memoria dei Lager nazisti nei racconti di duecento sopravvissuti.* Milan: Franco Angeli, 1986.

Bruzzone, Anna Maria. "Women in the Italian Resistance." In *Our Common History: The Transforma-*

tion of Europe, ed. Paul Thompson and Natasha Burchardt. Atlantic Highlands, N.J.: Humanities Press, 1982.

Bruzzone, Anna Maria, and Rachele Farina, eds. *La Resistenza taciuta.* Milan: La Pietra, 1976.

Calvino, Italo. *Il sentiero dei nidi di ragno.* Milan: Garzanti, 1987.

————. *The Path to the Nest of Spiders.* Trans. Archibald Colquhoun. New York: Ecco Press, 1987.

Colombo, Enzo. "Le opere e i giorni," In *Matrimonio in brigata: Le opere e i giorni di Renata Viganò e Antonio Meluschi,* ed. Enzo Colombo. Bologna: Grafis Edizioni, 1995.

Contadini e partigiani. [Acts from the conference Asti, Nizza Monferrato, December 14–16, 1984.] Alessandria: Edizioni dell'Orso, 1986.

De Grazia, Victoria. *How Fascism Ruled Women: Italy, 1922–1945.* Berkeley and Los Angeles: University of California Press, 1992.

D'Este, Carlo. *Bitter Victory: The Battle for Sicily, 1943.* London: William Collins Sons, 1988; reprint, New York: HarperPerennial, 1991.

Falaschi, Giovanni. *Realtà e retorica: La letteratura del neorealismo italiano.* Messina-Florence: Casa editrice G. D'Anna, 1977.

————. *La Resistenza armata nella narrativa italiana.* Torino: Einaudi, 1976.

Koon, Tracy H. *Believe, Obey, Fight: Political Socialization of Youth in Fascist Italy, 1922–1943.* Chapel Hill: University of North Carolina Press, 1985.

Spellanzon, Silvia. "Renata Viganò Poeta Popolare." In *Letterature moderne,* vol. 11, no. 6. Bologna: Cappelli Editore, 1961.

Vassalli, Sebastiano. "Introduzione a *L'Agnese va a morire.*" Turin: Einaudi Tascabili, 1974.

Viganò, Renata. L'Agnese va a morire. Turin: Einaudi, 1949.

————. *Arriva la cicogna.* Novara: Tipografia La Stella Alpina, for Editori Riuniti SpA of Rome: 1954.

————. *Donne della Resistenza.* Bologna: S.T.E.B., 1955.

————. *Matrimonio in brigata.* Milan: Vangelista, 1976.

————. "La storia di Agnese non è una fantasia." In *L'Unità,* November 17, 1949.

————. *Una storia di ragazze.* Milan: Cino del Duca, 1962.

Partisan Wedding

Partisan Wedding

Ciriaco, the owner, rose in a hurry to look for the commander. The house was small and black inside from the chimney smoke, and gray outside from the fieldstone. It shone at sunrise and at sunset and appeared flattened by the slate slabs held in place by large rocks so that the wind wouldn't carry them away. It was a house like so many others in the hills, and it was where they had put the brigade's command.

"Where is the commander?" said Ciriaco. He seemed a little agitated and uneasy, like he always was when he was forced to talk with that strange man who, although ragged, had the appearance of a gentleman and who was always first in duty and in danger. The partisan lookout sat on the bench and ate bread and cheese. The machine gun kept him company on the same bench, and at the first sign of trouble he would have given up breakfast.

"What do you want from the commander?" he asked. "Last night you didn't sleep at home; I saw you come up from the cliff. If you need to talk, go on up."

Ciriaco slanted his big shoes across the steps of the wooden staircase. He was so used to it that his feet knew the imprints on the planks of the steps.

"Commander Signor Renato," he said with confusion, entering the room that had been his nuptial chamber. Four partisans were sleeping on heaps of straw, but right away one of them raised his head.

"What is it?" he said. "What do you want?"

"I have only two words to say," responded Ciriaco. "Two words in secret."

The commander got up and shook the straw from his old suit. He was a man of medium stature, not too tall and not too small, with a rather handsome face, serious and unmoving; only his eyes were good and lively.

"Sleep," he said to the other three, who were stirring on the improvised beds. He went out with Ciriaco onto the landing of the stairway.

"I feel obliged to tell you," Ciriaco began, searching for the best words he knew, "that things are happening here that are not very good. I was happy to give you the house after having removed the furniture, my wife, my children. But if then something bad should happen, even to the house, I would be sorry."

The commander listened, but his way of tightening his jaw showed he was annoyed. In fact he said, "Try to hurry up with these words you want to tell me in secret."

And then Ciriaco made up his mind. "Again last night, White Moon went down to town. He goes to his girlfriend's, I think." He thought the commander would have shown some surprise or even anger; instead, he continued staring at him with his motionless face.

"You understand," said Ciriaco, by now forced to continue speaking, but also vaguely timid. "The Germans could discover him, or a *repubblichino* could follow him. After all," he repeated, catching the words like flies that were escaping him, "White Moon goes down every night to see a girl . . ."

"I didn't order you to report to me," said the commander.

Ciriaco turned his back on him, went down the stairs, and went outside. A summer morning; he heaved a huge sigh after the muffled hours of the night in the breath of the straw. "How beautiful!" he thought. "The field with the dewy grass, the tree branches bent by the weight of the chestnuts, the colors blue-gold-green. And we talk about painters! And these things we didn't know. Too bad that when this whole thing is over, we'll forget all about it." He stretched out his arms and yawned. "If we are still alive." He kicked a stone that bounced down the slope, striking the ground with dull, detached thuds. He concluded in a low voice, "Enough rhetoric. I need to talk to White Moon."

They were awakened by planes after the break in the neutral hour of dawn. They dropped bombs on a bridge; they were angry not to have destroyed it, and they'd been at it for some time now. Out of spite they made two circles on the village with the machine gunners out. But by now this was old hat; the people took refuge and nothing ever happened. The trouble would be for later, when the front passed, when the so-called Allies smashed everything until they were very sure they wouldn't meet up with a German face. In the midst of all this, between the Anglo-Americans sending up tons of iron and fire, and the fleeing Germans who vindicated themselves by killing whoever was in their way, were the defenseless population and the fighting partisans.

So many facts of life and death were still far away from that beautiful summer morning that had almost overwhelmed the commander Signor Renato. He resumed the business of everyday life, seating himself among the partisans to dunk bread in barley coffee, a kind of soup in which a spoon could stand straight up. And meanwhile he called out to Ciriaco, who had sat apart, by himself, in a touchy sulk typical of mountain people.

"Don't sulk," the commander said, and he hit him on the shoulder, and everyone made a fuss until even he felt like laughing.

"Here's White Moon," Legino suddenly yelled. He was the one who always saw farther than the others. The chestnut bushes at the foot of the large trees on the embankment moved, and White Moon appeared. He stopped suddenly because his companions on the bench all turned to look at him.

"Forward," said the commander, as if White Moon had knocked at a door. "Sit down, and give him a coffee."

He drank in a hurry and he put the bread in his pocket. It was clear that he wanted to speak, to explain. He managed to say "Commander Signor Renato" but Signor Renato in that moment was not in a mood to discuss. He gave the orders for the day and changed the guard, assigning the posts. Everyone rose, each one following his orders.

"You, too, Ciriaco, go cut your hay. Later, if one of the guys has time, he'll help you."

Now it was only White Moon with the commander. He looked around and it seemed as if the house and the field and the big, crooked chestnut trees on the edge of the precipice were no longer a familiar landscape, but an unknown, geometric formation, like something seen in a dream. "I . . . ," he said.

"You go to your girlfriend's place at night, I know," interrupted the commander. He paused, and the partisan's heart beat. "This can't go on, White Moon. You could have us all killed, with your carelessness."

White Moon's eyes were cast down and veiled. Perhaps he was about to cry, the impossible, rare tears of a man who has always shown himself to be smart and fearless.

"No one has died yet," said the commander with a slight shadow of a smile. "If you are sure about your woman, bring her up here; there is work for her, too."

"Thank you," stammered White Moon, "but she won't want to come; without a wedding, she won't want to come."

"We'll have a wedding," declared the commander. "I am here as a representative of the free government. In every brigade there is a commander who has the duty to die in action, if necessary, but also the authority to celebrate a wedding." This time he smiled with happiness: perhaps never in his life had he thought he would legally substitute for an official in a civil matter. "If you are sure of your woman," he repeated. The smile was gone. He wore the face of severe days, when his orders were free of comments and everyone obeyed even if they were not convinced, and then they realized that he always did what was right.

"I'll bring her," murmured White Moon. "I'm sure. But she is religious; she'd like to be married by a priest."

"Your lady likes too many things. Tell her that she can do without a priest," said the commander, "or do without you, and that if she doesn't come up and you go down another night, I'll move the formation and get rid of you. And then you'll really have to make other arrangements."

He saw the partisan Big Peter pass through the field: over six feet tall at age twenty-three, he weighed two hundred and fifty pounds.

"Big Peter," he called. The man came quickly, with the strange lightness that very large people can have. "Take Little Whistle with you, go into the house, and keep White Moon company so he sleeps in peace."

"In prison," said White Moon, and now he really began to cry.

"In peace," repeated the commander. "The day you go to take a wife, you should be fresh and rested, no?"

The night came with fresh dew on the grass, sweet silence in the rustling of the leaves. At the front there was a slow grumbling, and only the rays of the airplane reflectors cut through the sky waiting for the moon. The partisans went into action, four of them in one direction, five of them in another. They went down into the streets where the columns of German vehicles went by, and each time, they managed to leave a truck with its wheels in the air. The commander and his official, Caio, left for a mission about which they said nothing. Big Peter and Ciriaco stayed behind, Ciriaco who dared not move and who didn't sleep at night. Little Whistle had orders to take White Moon to town. At the clearing in the chestnut trees the fresh darkness came back, a background without voices. On the bench, Ciriaco was thinking about his life, his wife, his children, the furniture taken from the house, the house he'd tried to save, and who knew until when, and why; and who knew if they would be saved, if they would ever find themselves in the house again, like before . . . He gave a long sigh.

Big Peter finished eating a piece of bread. "Do you have a butt, Ciriaco? I'll give you one tomorrow. I think tomorrow we'll all be smoking. And don't sigh like it means nothing. What must be done will be done."

He went into the house to light the butt to avoid the wind that would have put out his match, and he returned to the bench with Ciriaco. Usually two partisans were on guard, but when it was Big Peter's turn they left him alone; he was so strong and attentive that he counted twice.

Everyone returned in the morning tired. Some found their bale of hay. There was a wire frame with a hair mattress for those who had worked the most, and the others slept in the hayloft. The last to arrive were Caio and the commander, and the formation began to worry. Although they had been on missions the entire night, the men couldn't sleep. As soon as they heard the voice and the footsteps coming down the path, they slept like stones. Now they were in peace; nothing had happened.

"Time to eat!" Tubby yelled full-voiced when the sun rose high on noon. The only functioning watch belonged to the commander, but Ciriaco took his cue from the light and seldom made a mistake. They got up, came out; the meal was ready: not great in quality, but enough in quantity. The easily satisfied didn't split hairs; no one suffered an upset stomach or complained about his liver.

They devoured it in joy, without a word. Hunger in the brigade was an enemy to combat in silence. Only when satiated, or almost, could they speak.

"And White Moon, where is he?" asked Rondò.

"And Little Whistle?" murmured Legino.

"Enough," said Gip, "the commander sent them into action."

But the commander heard the conversation. He wasn't far away, seated as he was on the ground to eat from his bowl. "They went to get the bride," he said. "Women take a while to fix themselves up."

Everyone laughed, thinking it was a joke, except the few who knew the truth.

"Here's White Moon," yelled Ciriaco from the top of the cliff. He had been silent lately and in a bad mood; all these things gave him too much to think about. White Moon was coming up through the chestnut trees, behind him was Little Whistle, and between them was a girl with a bundle in her arms. They came into the clearing, and Little Whistle joined his companions. He had performed his duty and now quickly picked up the bowl of food he had coming to him. So the couple was left standing there alone, White Moon at attention, the girl red as if her ears were on fire. The commander rose, went toward them, and said, "Put your things down. And congratulations."

He spun around and slowly walked across the field with his hands in his pockets. He turned and gave White Moon a cigarette, lighting it with the one he himself was smoking. "Tonight we'll have the wedding," he said. "Have you two eaten?" "Yes, yes," answered White Moon. He held the girl by the arm, his face was bright, cheerful, relaxed with happiness.

A great silence spread in the sun, and everyone stretched out to sleep here and there in the shelter of the trees. Only those on guard were awake, with a machine gun between their knees. And White Moon and the girl sat with their backs against the wall, speaking softly from time to time, not yet calm or persuaded of their adventure. The commander came from behind the house, looked at them with sympathy, and made a sign for them not to get up.

"What's your name?" he asked the girl.

"Marina," she responded.

"And what did you do in the village?" said the commander.

"I was a servant in a family of sharecroppers," murmured the girl. "I don't have any relatives. I'm an orphan."

She raised her eyes without fear, looking her questioner in the face with confidence, and smiled. He smiled, too.

"Cheer up! Now you're getting married. White Moon is a really great person."

The wedding was held at night; there was no moon, only stars shining in the dark sky. "Better to get married in the dark," said Big Peter, but the others begged him to be quiet. At that very moment, five bombers arrived in a flight pattern like birds. One silent and solitary plane dropped a Bengal light that opened sweetly. It was the usual maneuver used to bomb the bridge. The partisans ran to the edge of the field, where they could see the plain. The muffled explosions intensified with the whistles of nose dives, and again the useless explosions.

"Nothing doing," announced Legino. "Forty-eight times they've shot at us. They can't aim."

Everybody retreated nearer to the house, a dinner— a quick dinner, because there wasn't a lot to eat.

"I'm sorry that this wedding party is rather miserable," said the commander. "Here we don't have the bounty for two times in the same day. But a bottle for the bride and groom can be found. You can dig it up, can't you, Ciriaco?" He appeared to be in a good mood and his happiness spread through the group; everyone laughed and joked until he said, "We're ready."

They were gathered in a circle around White Moon and the girl.

"You are witnesses," pronounced the commander, his

voice with an unknown solemnity. He said, "Do you, man that we call White Moon, want to marry this woman that we call Marina?"

"Yes," answered the partisan, loudly.

"And do you, woman that we call Marina, want to marry this man that we call White Moon?"

"Yes," answered the girl, loudly.

"As representative of the free Italian government, I declare you united in matrimony," said the commander. "In due course, the documents will be filed."

He repeated, turning to the intense faces, "You are witnesses. With an oath." And to the bride and groom, "Embrace each other. I've finished."

He was amazed at himself for feeling extraordinarily moved—he who had always felt few emotions.

"Get going," he ordered. "Have a party. And Ciriaco, go get that bottle. You will drink it, owner of the house, with White Moon and Marina. To work, men: tonight we have stayed up a little late."

They weren't sorry to have Marina. She washed, ironed, did everything in the house. Of course the partisans envied White Moon when he went up to the attic with her. But the nights when it was his turn to work, White Moon was the most ready, and no one ever would have dreamed of offending his wife. Such was the law in the partisan formations—not a written law, but one felt in the conscience, and whoever disobeyed it faced a very severe punishment. Marina lived in this strange life, but it was a happy one for her since she had always suffered. Yes, she found herself in battle, every minute risking death, yet in a place where justice was already at work. Maybe she didn't realize the danger; the house seemed safe to her when she went to the barn, with White Moon or without White Moon. The only difference was to be seen as a woman, a wife. Until now the partisans had treated her as a being who worked only for her food. Sleep when one is tired is always welcome.

One day, she went with the hatchet to chop wood for the kettle. She was happy and singing. White Moon, who had been on duty that night, slept in his bed in the granary. "Tonight it's not his turn," thought Marina. She was sorry for the others when they went away, but certainly she was happy to have her husband at home. "Since I've been here, they've always come back," she reflected while putting her hand on the first branches. "Nothing has happened. It was worse down in the village, with the planes for the bridge, and the Germans." She remembered the bleak faces under the helmets; they all seemed the same to her. She didn't like them. One night one of them took her by the arm, "You, sweet love, come with me." She freed herself furiously and ran toward the house where she worked as a servant. In the kitchen, other Germans were seated, and she was afraid of running into "that one." She brought the pails of water, gave grass to the rabbits, sent the hens to the coop. Her day was over. "Come eat," yelled the lady of the house, but she fled to the pigsty where she had a cot; she threw herself upon it and fell fast asleep without eating.

"Here it's really altogether something else," she said aloud, since no one was around. And down she came with the axe; she had already made a good pile of wood. All of a sudden she had the impression that the leaves toward the bottom of the chestnut trees were moving; one moment, terror. And as she saw the Germans that were coming up the bank, she recognized multiple faces of the one who wanted to catch her for himself.

She threw the wood away and ran along the edge of the ditch. Her heart pounded in her throat, for fear that she wouldn't make it in time. She held the axe tight; it was a weapon. She understood in that moment what war is and that you can't put a weapon down in war. She arrived in the field panting heavily, yelling "The Germans, the Germans!"

The sentinel understood her and the alarm was sounded to the formation. She looked for White Moon; she didn't find him, as they all passed her by in a flash. She couldn't find even the commander. She threw herself to the ground behind the house with her head between her arms. She thought strange things, like "Why was the commander so quick?" and meanwhile she began to hear the shots.

Shots, shots: isolated, connected. They did not end; they filled the sky, the mountains, the trees. They assaulted her ears, they set her head on fire. She was laid out there as if she were dead; she didn't have the courage to look around her.

The attack was over. The partisans returned with hot guns, gathering in the clearing. No one was missing.

"Away, away," ordered the commander. "Now that they have found us, they'll arrive in force."

"Where's Ciriaco?" yelled Big Peter.

Ciriaco, terrorized, had hid himself in who knows what corner. He came out pale, his teeth chattering when he heard his name.

"It's useless to talk to him," said the commander. "He's incapable of understanding. Take him with you; we can't leave him behind."

Marina, on the other hand, had run to the known voices: she was clinging to White Moon.

"One of those Fritzes rolled down the hill there," said Legino. "I saw him go down like a sack." Legino's eyes didn't miss a trick.

"All the more reason to get out of here," responded the commander. "Fall into line on that path. The woman in the middle. Shake Ciriaco a little, and you, Leone, you have the canteen of grappa, try to give him a gulp. That'll wake him up. Tell him to think of the safest way to get to the other side of Monte Rocco toward San Gervaso delle Vigne. Move on."

The weak light of the sunset diminished. On the edge in front of them it was all sun. Here, already half dark. The partisans got ready in a hurry; they put as much stuff on their backs as they could and the rest they left, except for a little food and the weapons, all of which they took. The shadow made it suddenly dark, a really good time for a transfer. In the forest, under the branches, it was humid. Marina was cold in her light little dress, but she didn't risk stopping to take out her sweater from the tied bundle, which would have upset the entire line. Who knew where White Moon was—up front or in the back. She walked, trembling, still holding the axe handle tightly, with the bundle. "It can always come in handy," she thought, and between Big, who was in front of her, and Big Peter, who came behind her, she wasn't afraid at all.

They passed a rocky ford, and the entire company had to stop. There was the main road to cross.

"Out with the first ten," said the commander. "Expose yourselves as little as possible, and duck into the forest right away."

There was a quarter moon, small, but it lit the sky like a lamp. The road seemed white and shiny, and one could see everything even from far away. The ten, Ciriaco leading the way, threw themselves into the bushes of the crag. A space, silence.

"Forward another ten!" In a jump they were in.

"All together," ordered the commander, and he went. Behind him came three or four in a hurry, then Big and then Marina and the rest of the formation. And it was in that passage that they heard one solitary, mysterious discharge.

"Down, come on!" the last of them yelled, but as they ran away they saw Marina lying on the ground, on the street in the light of the moon. They grabbed her, they took her away, they disappeared. Legino, Gigio, and Vivolo stopped, pressing their machine guns to their eyelashes, and began to shoot in a burst of gunfire as if they were watering flower beds in a garden.

"Halt!" a yell from below. "Come down here."

A sound among the branches, a muffled murmur.

"We don't know where they are."

"We could be surrounded."

"Break out!" rang loud and clear the voice of the

commander. But down in the thicket they had come together in a group and one said, "They killed Marina."

"Break out!" repeated the commander. Right away
he ran forward, found White Moon, and stood in front
of him. He had been walking with the first ones who
were with Ciriaco, and had heard nothing but the shots.

"Are we there?" he asked.

The commander said, "Nothing. They made a mistake."

With fear, Ciriaco found the right path again. He got
back in line in the middle of the brambles and the large
trees. It was dark and fresh, a sense of security, of protection, of the good scent of the leaves. They couldn't
hear the footsteps on the soft ground of the chestnut
grove. The commander whispered to the man that
came before him, "Pass the word. Forward and silence."

And the voice passed from one to the other until the
last. Last came Big Peter, who carried Marina: white,
dead. In his arms she seemed like a sleeping child, and
he walked along crying, all covered in blood.

Peter

The evening he came to our house he was dead drunk. He knocked on the door during a downpour that filled the gutters with rainwater and poured down into puddles in the courtyard, making an enormous noise. I didn't want to open the door, but Diomira was afraid and said, "It's the Germans—they'll shoot us on the doorstep, on sight," and she ran to take the chain off the door. A soldier was leaning against the storm door, and as this gave way he came forward like a wave. In one step he was at the edge of the table, which he hit against and stopped.

"I'm Peter," he said. He was so small and drunk that he didn't scare me at all, even if he was dressed in a German uniform and had a rifle. Indeed, he was carrying the rifle in a very strange manner; it was hanging around his neck like a necklace and swinging under his throat from left to right, bumping the furniture and against the walls of the small, crowded room. On the other side of the thin, paneled wall, my husband, Antonio, and our baby were sleeping on a straw mattress, and in another bed nearby, with hardly enough space to get around it, were Diomira's husband and her little girl. We were all cramped together very tightly in a

43

peasant's farmhouse, in our assumed role of "refugees" from the city; but actually we were partisans.

It was hard being partisans in that village. It was the most obtuse, obscure group of houses and people I had encountered in my entire experience of the clandestine war. Diomira gave us shelter out of her love for money. Her husband, Serafino, was a bit better, a veteran of the war in Russia. He had an active, alert mind but was still enveloped in a fog of fears. Money and fear: these were the weights on the scale. Those two factors decided if the people in that town—even if they truly believed that we were fearful residents fleeing a bombed city—would take our side or that of the Germans.

And yet we were partisans, and Antonio commanded the brigade—companies of men lost among the water and the fog, to whom we ferried supplies and the means to live by boat from our insecure base. November 1944, in the valleys of the Ferrara lowlands.

"Me Ruski," Peter said, his rifle almost striking me in the face.

I dodged the black hole of the barrel, because a drunk can easily fire a shot, and I asked him if he wanted a drink. On principle I always gave a drink to whoever came into that room that was so important to our existence, if they were friends or enemies, Germans or Italians, people of our faith or suspected spies.

"Me P. W.," Peter wrote on the table with a finger dipped in wine, and he added by voice, "Prisoner of the *doich*."

Serafino must have heard from his bed. "Who's there?"

I answered, "A Russian," and he got up and came out. He found himself in front of Peter in the light of the gas lamp. They looked at each other a bit, and it seemed to me they recognized each other. But no, they had never seen each other. It was only that in Russia, Peter had seen many like Serafino, and Serafino many like Peter.

Then Serafino dragged from his memory a few labored words of Russian. Peter's face—a small, round face with a rolled mustache, drawn with features so happy that it would have seemed funny and smiling even when at risk of death—became even more gay; happiness made man.

"Let him go!" said Diomira. "Get him out of here. If the Germans come . . ."

"To hell with the Germans!" Serafino shouted. He was excited, happy like Peter. Memories of the most desperate and lucky adventure of his life killed off his present fear. The dialogue was reduced to names of cities, rivers, and towns, pronounced by Serafino: the sad itinerary of the retreat, covered with death, each name a flame of childlike joy for Peter. His enthusiasm was such that it was translated into hugs. Stalingrad! A hug. The Don—a hug, Dnepropetrovsk—a hug, Kiev—a hug. It was the same road, and they had both taken it, one in front who was escaping, the other following behind, chasing him, and then, about-face. And the one in front was escaping and the other was chasing him. Both of them could smell again the odor of mud, the odor of the snow, the odor of death, the odor of Russia —the beautiful things and the ugly things, the joy and the pain of each and every one of them in that same, immense country. Both of them, the Italian and the Soviet, in their nostalgia, missed the same lands—one who would have liked to have seen them again in peace-time, the other who feared he would never see them again.

"What's going on?" Antonio asked from his straw bed, awakened by the sound of Peter's rifle, knocking about in that careless rejoicing.

"Nothing," I answered. "It's a Russian, prisoner of the Germans. He wanted to come in."

"Give him something to drink," my husband ordered.

I answered, "But he's already dead drunk."

"Give him something to drink anyway," he concluded. He was exhausted from the dark day, soaked by the valley, and he turned his face to the wall, jealous of the few hours conceded to sleep.

I poured wine into a glass; Peter looked at it against the light. He reached it out to Serafino, he lifted it and lowered it like a priest at Mass, and he emptied it in one gulp. It was his way of making a toast dedicated to one special person.

"Me guard," he said, laughing so you could see his teeth shining through his mustache and his light eyes through his lashes. "Horsey guard."

"You're in here and watching the horses?" Serafino said, a bit in Russian, a bit in Italian, and with lots of gesticulating.

"*Doich* good . . ." Peter cautiously announced. "Italiani good, not crook. Everyone sleep. Me free," and he started to laugh hard, like a child who's played a trick.

"Even horsey sleep," he added and he extended the glass so that it could be refilled.

"Enough already, for the love of God!" Diomira interrupted. "Get him out of here or he'll drink all our wine."

I, too, said "Enough" and took the flask away.

But Peter wasn't of a mind to go yet; he pointed to the wooden partition with his finger, his face like a question mark. "My husband and the children—sleeping"; I showed him, putting my hands aside my head. "I to see" said Peter, innocent, imploringly. He ventured forth into the tight opening where a curtain acted as a door, pushing it with the butt of the rifle.

"But what the hell is going on?" Antonio shouted. "Will you let me sleep?"

"Me *tovarish*"* the Russian murmured, and Serafino went in there, too. He told him something we didn't understand, and then Peter threw himself onto the bed, still with his bulky rifle. He hugged Antonio, kissed the sleeping child, and started again with hugs and his litany of names: "Stalingrad . . . Kharkov . . . Kiev . . ." Serafino had whispered to him that the man in the bed had also been in the war in Russia. We all laughed, but by now the fun had gone on a bit too long. We took the soldier, each one taking an arm, and brought him back to the kitchen. He finally persuaded himself that it was late, that we wanted to sleep. Before going out, he

* Comrade.

pulled us close, showed us a wide smile, a white opening in the black of his mustache, and said quietly as if
he were giving us a gift: "I'm not Peter—Petruscia.
Peter for *doich*."

He threw himself out into the rain. We heard him
gallop away like a horse in the water that was inundat-
ing the courtyard.

We saw him often in the neighborhood near a house
where the Germans had a food camp. Somehow, he managed always to do nothing for them, with his air that was
half foolish and half drunk. They called him to load the
carts; he ran to place two hands under the weight, groaning and moaning. But he really wasn't expending any energy at all; the stuff was lifted up by the Germans that
were up on the cart. And so he would go, "Uuusshh," a
sign of satisfaction, of relief, as if all the effort had been
his own. Then he started to sing and dance his national
dance, becoming a dancing ball on two little legs of rub-
ber. The Germans laughed, putting their hands on their
foreheads to say he was crazy. They didn't treat him badly.
Only Otto followed him with his glance. Otto the
Berliner, the Nazi, who watched us a lot, too, and the disproportionate supply of rations that came the way of our
small family, and the great quantity of visits from people
not from the village, strange for refugees from the city.

"You to know whole town," he said to me one day,
slowly.

I was quick to reply, "Black market," without specify-
ing if we were the ones buying or selling.

He turned on his heel without saying anything else:
he didn't have orders to do so, so he let it go. He was an

authentic type, the real, generic "German invader," stupid and clever and cruel all at the same time. He only did what he was commanded to do, and he did it heavily, with evil, meticulous as an accountant. Nothing else mattered to him.

He let it go, even the time that he brought me an enormous, live goose, stolen from who knows where, and he ordered me to kill it and pluck it. Aside from the fact that I was not capable of killing any type of fowl, I was certainly not there to pluck geese for the Germans. So I told him that I had injured my shoulder during a bombardment, that I couldn't move my arm. Peter was there, staring at me with his shining eyes. Even Otto fixed his stare on me. He made an insulting gesture, hitting the goose in the head, and he went away dragging the screaming goose behind him.

"You good," Peter said to me quickly, and he added some words in his own language.

"*Dosvidania,*"[†] he whispered, before running toward Otto and grabbing the goose by the neck. He put himself to work pulling out the feathers, but that day he avoided coming near the ramshackle shed that served as our house.

The German subsistence camp was about to break. We noticed it from certain preparations, from an unusual movement of men and vehicles. Peter seemed to be erased. Serafino watched him from afar, and Peter would go away quickly.

† Farewell.

"There are also Russian prisoners ready and armed for an antipartisan action. You need to be careful," Serafino said. He was a little disappointed. Maybe he didn't believe it much, but we had plenty of other worries and responsibilities, and we had little time or inclination to worry ourselves about Peter. Antonio left every day in a boat, and I prepared the baskets and the bags of food, and the extra difficult supplies of socks, scarves, and sweaters for the winter that by now had extended its icy presence over the pale, dull water of the valley. I had help from the women comrades who came kilometers and kilometers by bicycle to gather from one base and bring to another the things that were extremely needed. This was what we did from the time that the Anglo-American advance had stopped, parking itself for the winter. Alexander's proclamation had postponed everything to spring.

It was early one morning, as I was in the courtyard getting water at the pump, when Serafino appeared next to me, white and agitated.

"The Germans are leaving tonight," he said, "and Peter doesn't want to go with them."

Truthfully, with so much to do, right at that moment I didn't know what he was talking about.

"Yes, Peter the Russian, he wants to escape, to stay with us."

I let the pail fill to overflowing on the wall. "But Antonio is not here; how can we decide? How can we trust him?" I remembered all of a sudden Peter's face when he said *"Dosvidania"* to me, with his serious eyes, and then we never saw him again, hanging around drunk between the house and the courtyard.

"I'll try to reach Antonio, to ask for orders," I said. "Without him, I can't do anything."

And so Serafino, who had never had the courage to make a decision, at least since I'd known him, and who lived in fear of everything, told me this amazing thing: "If you don't want him, I'll take Peter, I'll hide him. In the retreat from Russia, I would have died, too, if I hadn't found . . ." He couldn't go on: he was a man of few words, not given to emotion. What he had to say, he'd said. Peter had to stay.

"I'll send a *staffetta*," I said, getting the pail and my calm back together. "I know, luckily, that Antonio is not far."

I went away quickly with my child. It was a day in December, a white sky, but without snow or fog, as there are in the hard winters of the valley. The cold bit and burned, but we were used to it; we breathed that bitter, colorless air without damage. The baby was covered well—he was having fun, he was happy. I, much less well-covered, found warmth in the frenzy. I soon saw the woman comrade I was looking for; she left, pressing hard on the pedals. I knew that in a few hours I would have an answer. Upon my return, the courtyard was full of cars, trucks, Germans hurrying around, but in my shed there was no one. The lit stove was beautiful, the coals soon becoming hot and red, and even the little meal with the baby gave me a sense of happiness in my excitement.

In the afternoon I learned that Diomira had gone with her daughter to see her mother in a small town nearby. It seemed like a good idea; maybe it was

Serafino's idea, but I didn't bother to find out. I was awaiting Antonio's orders, and I watched the activity of the departure from the window in the door. Peter was nowhere in sight, and neither was Serafino. I wondered what I would do if I didn't see anyone again, not even the *staffetta* I'd sent to Antonio. But she was the first to arrive, a fast, blond girl, about whom I knew only her combat name, "Nadia." She told me that Antonio agreed to keep the Soviet soldier. He would come later; he hoped he'd get here in time to help me, but otherwise I'd have to avail myself of Serafino. She repeated his message exactly: "In this particular case, you can trust Serafino."

Indeed, when the company began to load the vehicles and cars, Peter was there in full action, working with the others. He stopped a moment at my door, and he seemed to me extraordinarily changed: in perfect form, sober and serious, he was clean, dignified in his long German overcoat, with the letters *PW* stamped clearly on one side of his chest. Serafino came, too, with the latest information. The company was leaving in that vague hour between day and darkness, when the English airplanes that we generically called "Pippo" would have stopped their usual air raids because of the uncertain light. Even Peter would be leaving with the Germans. Then, in the black of night, he would let himself slip down from a car and come back. I was to wait for him in the street that ran along the canal and conduct him to the valley guards at the big house, which had been abandoned by the poaching surveillance and then converted into our rapid refuge. It was on the edge of the flooded valley, and it was where the boats for the partisan transports docked.

"Two small boats will come, and they will sing like little valley birds. Peter will go with them."

I said, "Good. But you, Serafino, have to stay with my son in the house; don't leave him even for a minute, unless Antonio comes."

"Of course," he answered. "It has to appear to be a regular evening, like all the others."

Like all the others! An unvoiced anguish seized me thinking of the long wait, and of what would happen if the Germans found out about the escape. Just like calm soldiers given the task of subsistence or raiding the livestock, they would become Nazi beasts, unleashed in revenge. Otto would take command, with those cold colorless eyes of his, his lacerating and inexorable voice.

My son was already asleep by the time I went out into the empty courtyard after the noisy departure of the cars. It was darker than I'd expected, and it was difficult for me to gain access to the bridge and turn into the small road that ran among the fields and water. The wet cold of the swamp was like an icy blanket on my shoulders, but I didn't know if the drops on my forehead were from the fog or my own sweat. I felt I was in a bath that was both icy and burning; I clenched my hands together and didn't feel them, as if they weren't mine. Time no longer mattered; it could have been an hour or a century. There I was in the right place; in front of me, the narrow street, and an expanse of black fields with a few tree branches printed against a sky that was slightly less black. Silence, immobility, a few splashes in the water, a small noise, maybe a stone or who knows what. The valley, both at night and during the day, is never completely still and silent.

Then little by little came a rumbling, a crackling of ice frozen in the furrows of the carriages, and a shadow came along in the dark. I waited until what was making the sound got close enough that I could smell the odor of the barracks in his clothes. It was a small man. "Peter?" I said, and he answered me, *"Da."* It could just as easily have not been him, but in those moments one doesn't stop to think. Fear dissolves, disappears, and if then an error that might even be fatal happens, there is nothing left but a great amazement. That time it was really him, and I took him by the hand. We walked without talking along the furrows of the frozen street, careful to make no noise. It wasn't more than a kilometer, but it felt like we were making our way for an entire night. The time and the cold no longer made sense. I saw in a flash the dark profile of the big house and distinguished the smell of the valley water. Almost immediately a gurgling whistle rose, one heard so many other times on those ridges, when the birds flew by. The boat was there, alongside the short border of the embankment.

"Ehilà,"‡ one of the partisans said under his breath, and he jumped up near us.

"Antonio sends us," I murmured. "Bring him to the base."

‡ Hello there.

"Me Petruscia, with rifle," the Soviet announced, as if showing his identity papers.

"Dosvidania," I told him, while the partisan guided him down the muddy border to the boat. Very softly I heard the stroke of the oar on the riverbank, and then the murmur of the sliced water. They are long boats, silent, fast, useful for poaching. I stayed and listened. There was nothing more to hear. So I turned back, and this time the road seemed extremely short, a few, quick steps as I beat a path to the warm room where I found Serafino on guard and my son, who had never awakened.

The Portrait of Garibaldi

Mario got on his bicycle and said good-bye to the comrade on the bridge. The May sunset was slowly dying; the glass shone in the windows of the houses scattered among the fields. It seemed there was no war in that green and gilded hour of the valley, with the pale fog that began to creep up from the marshes. Mario stopped the pedals, coasting rapidly down the slope, rustling on the worn tires. The street had become gray and deserted, and he looked at the color of the asphalt, recognizing it for having followed it so many times, like the floor of his room. He thought meanwhile about the hard day that had passed, full of risks for the clandestine work, and about so many other hard days that would have to pass before the Anglo-Americans, continuing up the Italian peninsula, arrived in the northern provinces occupied by the Germans and Fascists. He found himself humming in the rhythm of the pedals: "They go slow slow slow, who knows when we will see them." Distracted, suddenly, he saw the wall of the house to the right. He braked, putting one foot on the ground.

At that moment, a flash and a noise hit him, and all thought in him was extinguished. He fell forward with his arms outstretched, and the bicycle hurtled away on impact, almost to the middle of the street. He remained there, motionless, with his face against the step of his door. A moment of silence, heavy like lead. Then from the house men and women came. From one of the women rose a very high-pitched wail that was lost in the echo. The others ran crying and screaming, but the street filled with armed soldiers, rigid faces, hands ready on machine guns. And they immediately drove the group back with short cries: *"Raus, Raus."* The men scattered; they were all either old or boys, and the women dragged them away. The woman who was wailing remained, prostrate on the ground near the body but without touching it. She covered her eyes with her hands, and then tried to look, and then yelled again louder.

"Enough," said a voice suddenly. It was one that commanded the herd, and he came closer, to touch the dead man with his foot. With his foot he grazed the woman also. She jumped up sharply, hitting her fists on the gray cloth of the uniform; she clung to the material of the black shirt. He gave her a push that sent her slamming against the wall. He ordered his men, "Turn him over."

They grabbed the dead man by the shoulders and turned him over. Underneath him there was a large stain of blood; his head, which had not been hit, fell into the middle of that blood. His face seemed disfigured, but it was oddly intact. Roughly, they kicked him toward the house and two of them sat down on the step with their machine guns between their knees.

"Here, and no one move," yelled the boss, raising his voice toward the windows. "And away with the woman."

They picked the inert woman up and pushed her against the door; someone opened it and pulled her inside. The other Blackshirts followed the sharp order, *"Raus."* The last one gave the bicycle a kick that sent it meandering, and it overturned in the ditch. It was almost dark and cool in the evening; from inside the house came laments and soft cries. The voices of the armed soldiers resounded loudly from afar, in sync with their marching step, imitating German words. In Italy they spoke like the Germans, they acted like the Germans, but they were, unfortunately, Italian Fascists.

A boy first brought the news to the town. He had run away behind the house, and he had waited, hidden in a field. When night fell, he slid down from the bank of the river, passed the railroad bridge, and reached a place where he was certain not to run a risk. He knocked a special knock on the door; inside, they understood and came right away, although it was already past the hour of the curfew. In the kitchen, the family was close and reunited in the light of the candle. They were already in a state of alarm because they had heard the sound of firing from the faraway countryside. "They killed Mario," said the boy, almost hoarse. A woman offered him a chair and he sat. He put his elbows on the table, and he bent his head as if he were falling asleep.

A man near the chimney got up, pacing two or three steps forward and back, stopped and caressed his hair.

"The Germans?" he murmured.

The boy turned his face up suddenly to look at him, and his eyes filled with tears. "No, not the Germans," he replied. "It was the Fascists, the Blackshirts. There was also Eros di Masino. People from our own town."

A young man seated at the table spit on the ground and made a muffled moan, squeezing his fists.

"Silence," imposed the old man. "Something must be done here. Otherwise they'll take us all like that, like mice." He turned to the young man.

"You, Armandino, tonight go sleep in the barn. Go deep inside, into the hay, and don't come out until I call you. You others, Genoveffa and Debora, as soon as the curfew is over, you'll go on an errand; I'll tell you where and to whom." He interrupted himself because his wife Nina began to cry softly, her face turned toward the dark corners of the room.

"What is it? Are you crying? Don't you remember anymore when you carried the red flag during the strikes, Giumenta?" He always called her that, using the name of a horse, not as an insult, but with affection, as if to tell her she was good and faithful. And at that name she rubbed her eyes and said, "Me, you know I'm not afraid, Brando. It's fear for the children."

"I'm leaving now," said the boy who had brought the news. He was almost sorry he had come. But the man grabbed him by the arm.

"Does your mamma know that you're here? Good. You go, too, with Armandino to the barn. You can't go home. Tomorrow morning I'll take care of it."

Throughout the night he thought about it, awake in his bed next to his wife, who was also awake. Without a word, they passed the hours until the first light whitened the window. They went down to the kitchen together, as they had in the days of enormous summer work, and she hurried to prepare the breakfast. This way they were all ready in a few minutes, and Brando told them what they had to do. Genoveffa and Debora took their bicycles and left on the carriage road; they were young, dark-haired, and dark-skinned. They looked so much like each other, they could have been twins.

Nina went out into the courtyard and fed corn to the chickens. As she stood in the middle of the vast circle of land, she assured herself that the surrounding fields and the street down the hill were deserted and tranquil. Even the town was quiet. The sun came up clearly in the May morning.

"Okay," said Brando, and he, too, went by bicycle, with the boy on the handlebars. He left him at the end of the carriage road before he turned between the tufts of brush toward home.

"Go and hide," he advised. "Check first that there are no more Blackshirts. Try to see Tonio the blacksmith and tell him to come to me later." He left quickly, pushing the pedals, and he turned to be sure that the boy had understood. He felt as agile and strong as he had so many years ago, when the Fascist squadrons had first hunted him down, caught him, and beaten him uselessly.

The Blackshirts were still around. Mario's death was decreed and carried out as "an example," they said. That is, to demonstrate with actions what fate awaited all those who even dreamed of going against the Germans and the Fascists. So for twenty-four hours Mario lay as he had been cut down by the burst of fire, stretched out there in the blood, all night, with his face turned toward the stars, all one long day under the sun. Cries and screams were of no use; neither wife nor mother was listened to. The house was guarded by armed men, and no one was to touch the body. People passed by on the street and the guards with their rifles shouted, "Get Away! *Raus!*" But not too many people passed by. Women, girls, old folks, just those who couldn't refrain from looking, those who risked the least. It was understood by now that this scene hadn't been created "as an example": the atrocity of leaving a cadaver out in plain view was an act of provocation. It was a challenge; a way to attract a scared or exasperated crowd and then to suddenly do a round-up: choose the healthy men, escort them, and push them ahead under the threat of death toward who knows what destination, a concentration camp or forced labor, risking the lives of all, and securing a sure death for whoever even thought of rebelling.

Only toward nightfall, during the same, quiet hour in which the hedges began to be damp and dark with long shadows under the slanting rays, the Blackshirts rose to their feet, keeping their loaded rifles by their sides and marching in a line toward the town. The last two marched backwards, close together, keeping the house and the road in view. Not a sound was heard from the house, but there was the force of a held-back strength inside its walls, a bomb on the point of exploding, contained by the authority of those who knew better and by the desperate energy of the weakest ones. A quivering silence; and for a little while longer the body remained alone by the wall. Then everyone came out, and finally actions and words were freed. Tears fell and dried on hot, tired faces.

Mario was himself again, but dead. They lifted him, they brought him to his room, they washed the dried blood from his face and hair, they put on his Sunday suit. In the house, behind the doors and windows, there was a whisper, a rustle, a desolate sound. Mario was not only a young man, good, loved by his family, but he was also a leader, a director of the anti-Fascist struggle, the most important leader and director of that valley zone where a Garibaldian formation was being created. And so the night passed, made quiet and inoffensive by the Nazi curfew, that was made of iron like their helmets, and that guarded the weapons.

In the morning, all the towns and villages and the scattered houses in the countryside were warned. It was like a flame in the stubbles and on the moors: it begins in a point and right away gains ground; it goes, it runs, turns, goes back again only to find new life. Only it finds more arid offshoots, and slowly it becomes a vast burning terrain, one not easy to enter, where it is even harder to get out unscathed. In the plains, people came and went on old bicycles that the Germans had no need of, and the new ones were kept hidden so they wouldn't be taken away. But even the tires and the worn wheels went fast under the thrust of strong legs, and it was no problem if your forehead or arms sweated with the effort. "Whatever needs to be done, let it be done, and the rest is of no matter," said the men and women from house to house. And the "rest" could even be death.

There were, however, those on the side of the Fascists, and it wasn't clear what advantage or profit they derived from it. They'd always worked like everyone else, and they found themselves at war like everyone else, yet they let themselves be tricked by mirages and promises that, while not kept in twenty years of government, had even less chance of being maintained now by a broken government. Fortunately, there were few of them, and in general they were more stupid and ignorant than capable of betrayal, even though in hard times like this, even ignorance and stupidity can end up in betrayal.

By afternoon Mario was in the coffin in the middle of the kitchen, which had been stripped of its furniture. It was a large room, with space for him and all those who wanted to see him. And everyone went—women, old folks, children, men, and even those who could have been recognized and taken and held hostage in the guerrilla war. In the springtime afternoon, on the streets hit by the sun, in the troubled neighborhoods, in the middle of the dull voices in the small groups of people gathered together, the Fascists weren't there, the Nazis weren't there. They had burrowed into the barracks or the Fascist headquarters, playing cards and drinking, pretending nothing had happened. But that crowded murmur, those muffled steps, that rebellion compressed to the extreme margins of caution in the solid interest of avoiding the worst and of not wasting force and human lives, held the Nazis and Fascists in a confused climate of uncertainty and fear.

Mario was there in the coffin, raised slightly at the end where his head lay. His stomach and abdomen were swollen and taut; his face seemed smaller, dark, his eyes weighted closed by his thick, dark eyelashes. He appeared as in his most burning hours, when he spoke to the comrades at the meetings, four, five, or six of them, gathered in a stable, or sitting on the bank of a ditch. Sometimes in a passionate discussion, he closed his eyes, searched for the word inside himself, found the way to express himself so the others would be persuaded. Now he was silent, immobile; and tomorrow he would be buried. Yet his place did not remain empty: ten, one hundred, one thousand continued on that road. The Fascists never understood this, and the Nazis even less. It was their great mistake, and it cost them the war.

Brando returned just in time for curfew. The family gathered in the kitchen, barred the door, and closed the windows. Outside, in the middle of the dark landscape, you could barely see the isolated house. They were safe together, inside.

"Good," said Brando, and sat down at the table. Everyone looked at him, waiting, and he smiled a slow smile among the wrinkles of his peasant face.

"There are partisans in the valley," he announced. "We'll make a Garibaldian brigade, and we'll name it after Mario."

He cut a fat slice of bread and began to eat peacefully. There was some rabbit stew, and Nina rose to serve it.

"You, too, will join the brigade, Armandino," said Brando after a while. "There at least something can be accomplished. Here you could die without even knowing it."

"Yes, Daddy," replied Armandino, and even his mother and his sisters nodded their heads.

"You two," continued Brando, turning to his daughters, "will work with Bernardo. I've already talked to him about it. We need blankets, beds, safe places, something to eat . . . ," he stopped a moment to reflect. "And tomorrow I will go to see Eligio della Marana."

Nina froze. "That one will want nothing to do with it," she said. "I know him well."

Brando rose, placing an arm around his wife's shoulders. He had a tired and affectionate voice.

"Don't be afraid, Giumenta. I know how to talk to him, to Eligio. To him and to many others."

Genoveffa and Debora chattered softly, laughing. It seemed as though they might have something to say. And finally Debora spoke, nudging Genoveffa's arm.

"But Gianna, Eligio's daughter will work with us, too. I know for sure. I ran into her yesterday. She was going to bring the soup to the boys hidden in the Casa Rossa."

"Good," said Brando. He carefully took an ember from the fireplace; he needed it to light his pipe. He took a deep breath, caught up in the pleasure of the smoke.

And at sunrise he was already on his bike headed toward his friend Eligio's house. They had been childhood friends because they had grown up together, but then they had lost touch due to political differences. Eligio did not want any trouble; in 1921 when the Fascists beat Brando to a bloody pulp, he pretended not to know anything. He no longer even showed his face around town. Late at night he went to see Brando, and he would find him covered with bruises, or with a swollen eye, or with skin broken from blows with a club. Then they discussed and argued, but nonetheless he helped Nina with the compresses and the medicines, and in the end they made peace. Now, it had been awhile since they had seen each other, because Eligio, with the German and Fascist occupation, had renewed his fear.

"Hello," Brando said, on the threshold of the kitchen. It was a nice kitchen, large and comfortable, with tiled floor, a radio, a gas oven, even a refrigerator. Brando knew that even though his friend worked the land, he could call himself well-off.

"Good morning," replied Eligio and Selene, his wife, without much enthusiasm. But right away Eligio felt the discomfort of his own coldness, and he rose saying, "Come in, come in; so what brings you here after so much time? . . ."

Brando did not let him finish. "I've had too much to do," he replied. "But today I have to talk to you."

He looked at Selene intently, to make her understand that she should leave. She took a basin full of washed clothes under her arm and went out to hang the laundry on the line in the middle of the courtyard.

But she did not seem happy nor attentive to her work; she turned around every once in a while to look at the two men through the opening of the door. She wasn't able to make out the words. She only saw the many sharp, determined gestures, and the faces close together and hot from the discussion. At a certain moment Brando got up, and Eligio too; they both stared at a point on the kitchen wall. Selene was not able to understand what it was. Then once again they made gestures and spoke together, and she could no longer resist. She sat herself down behind the shutter, pressed against the wall, and listened.

"Garibaldian partisans," Brando was saying. "Have you understood what a Garibaldian brigade is?"

Eligio still raised his eyes toward that point on the wall,

"Yes, yes, yes," urged Brando. "It's like the other time, when Garibaldi passed by here with Anita pregnant and sick, and he stopped to eat in this very house and everyone here in the valley got cracking. Your grandfather told us. He was here, your grandfather, in this house, when Garibaldi passed by with Anita. And not many kilometers away, a big town on the sea is called Porto Garibaldi, and it was because the Garibaldini had to land on that beach followed by the Austrian ships. And inland, so close that from your yard you can see the roofs, there's a little town called Anita, because Anita died there. Garibaldi made Italy with his Garibaldini, and even your grandfather followed him, and my grandfather, and so many of our elders. Now we must save all that we can, and here we are, the sons and grandsons of Garibaldi, and the enemy is still the same, or at least it still looks the same."

Only Brando was speaking, and Eligio was there listening to him. It seemed to him that never in his life had Brando made such a long speech. And he also recognized that he was right. He looked up as he had before, and Selene finally understood that it was the portrait of Garibaldi that he was staring at, an old print that everyone in and outside that house had always seen hanging on that wall. Then she went in as if she had been called and sat with them at the table.

"What do I have to do?" Eligio asked in a very low voice.

"For now, hide some of the draft dodgers. You will keep them with your son Ermes. I know that for some time he's been living in the cellar. Even deeper than the cellar, where you find water if you dig. When the time is right, we will come to get them, to join the brigade. It's not healthy to stay down there for months in that darkness with your feet all damp. Then we'll see each other, or I will send you a message through one of my daughters."

There was an oppressive, heavy silence. Each person thought about the grave things that had been said, and about the other, even more grave things that would be done.

"Uncork a bottle," said Eligio to his wife. "Give Brando a glass."

There was no happiness in that order, only an ancient habit, the sign of hospitality.

"And I must also tell you," said Brando slowly, "that your Gianna is a *staffetta* with the partisans."

Eligio and Selene stood still, looking at the mouth that had pronounced those words. It was as if they did not believe it.

"I know it seems strange," said Brando. "She's small, blond, shy. Yet she is the best, the most courageous."

He took the glass that Selene had poured him, but he didn't drink it.

"Our brigade will be named after Mario," he continued in the same voice, almost a monotone. "It will be the best way to remind us of how they killed him, and to continue what he wanted."

Selene passed a handkerchief across her face, wiping away two long, shining lines of tears, and Eligio responded, "Bring the boys here, and when you take them away, take my Ermes from the cellar, too," he swallowed. His throat was almost closed: "You're right, it's dark and wet down there . . ."

Brando drank his glass, slowly, and threw the last drop on the ground, as is done among the country folk. All three of them remained in silence, with sweaty and pale faces, looking beyond the opening of the door at the great morning light.

Campalbo

The dawn came up along the side of the mountain, exposing the opposite slope and sending a blast of wind into the red, hard leaves of the little beech tree on the overhanging rock. The slanting light shone into the fields on the brown slices of overturned earth, drinking the dew from the grass.

Only in the little town at the end of the big valley was it still dark. The town bridged a silent torrent, and at this hour enjoyed its most beautiful hour of sleep before beginning another hard day of war and suffering.

The first one to open the door was Scangina. She went to the fountain with her pail to get some water and returned in a hurry. In the kitchen she could hear a strange squeaking, the springs of a bed that were trembling, and a spine-shivering moan, as if from someone who has a great chill and whose teeth chatter without stopping. It was Geo, her son, who had come home from Greece with tuberculosis and malaria, who just this morning had had an attack. "Of all mornings," he stuttered with effort between the huge shaking that wracked his body with fever, "and there are the newspapers to bring up to the brigade."

He was fiery red up to his forehead, with his eyes

wide open and dull, like a corpse. But his mother didn't fret; by now she had seen him many times like this.

"What can we do, what can we do," Geo complained. "And 'they' are waiting."

Gelinda came down the wooden stairs, awakened by the voices.

"Is Geo feeling bad? I'll go up to Campalbo for the papers," she said. She threw back the hair that kept falling in her eyes. Her hair was brown with blond streaks bleached by the sun. She went to wash up with the cold water from the pitcher.

"Really, Mom," she insisted. "Tell Geo that he can relax. I know how to do it."

She put her little dress on and combed her hair in front of the glass of the window. She was a serious girl for her thirteen years, with the many misfortunes that she had already suffered. She still remembered her dad, when he was taken by the Germans in a roundup, how they threw him in prison in the capital of the province, how she and her mother went many days to bring him food to eat, walking the sixteen kilometers. One time they met the chaplain of the prison and they asked him, crying, if they could see Daddy. And the chaplain had to tell them how he had been shot the night before, with nine others, as retaliation.

Her mother stood still, thinking, and she passed behind Geo's curtain. By now his fever was very high and had given him the chills and taken away his consciousness.

"I'm no good for going to Campalbo," she said with

tears in her eyes. "And here in this filthy town, who can we trust, who?"

"Me!" Gelinda insisted, and she gave her mother a rough kiss. "No shoes, I'll be even faster. I'll go over to Discaro's to get the stuff."

She ran away, barefoot, small on the street that was light with the day.

She didn't run into anyone and arrived at Discaro's place just as he was opening the shed where he worked as a shoemaker. He was fat and half hunchbacked, by dint of pulling the thread, but for firearms he was fine. He had left one of his legs behind in Albania.

"I came to get the papers for the brigade. Geo has the fever again. I'll go to Campalbo," Gelinda said all in one breath. She was afraid Discaro would say no.

Instead he looked at her in his way, screwing up one eye. "Fine," he said. "We have no choice."

He gave her a little shopping bag with two cheeses. "This is the excuse for those damned nosy ones down in the valley." Then he lifted up a stone from the floor and took out a bundle of papers, not too big. "And this, where will you put it?" he said, worried.

"Where do the others put it?" the girl asked.

Discaro smiled. "Good God, the men in the big bag, the women down their shirts."

"Give me some string," Gelinda said. He gave it to her, and turned away out of respect. She bustled, fussed, and tied it. "Well, no one will notice anything!" they exclaimed together when she had finished.

"And another thing," he said. "Keep in mind: as soon

as you see *them,* you have to say 'Sheep and wolf, Discaro sends me.'"

Off she went down the road, Gelinda with her little shopping bag of cheeses. And she needed them, too, because she ran into a gossip who asked her where she was going. "On an errand for my mother," she answered, contrite. But as soon as she was out of sight, she entered the woods and got on the ridge. It was difficult but surer. She climbed up like a goat. Once in a while she touched her stomach to feel the paper crackle. She had been to Campalbo many times, years earlier with her girlfriends. It was a beautiful summit of rocky mounts, and they used to get up there in a moment, laughing and screaming. This time the way up was longer, so much so she feared she'd taken the wrong road. But soon after that she recognized the rocks, and with the final slope, the hardest one, she emerged onto the soft and marshy field. She dried her sweat and ran in the soaking grass toward a man that was filling a bucket patiently at the trickle of the spring's source. She said, "Sheep and wolf, Discaro sends me." He dropped the bucket from the surprise, and she added, "I've got the papers. Geo my brother has a fever. He couldn't come."

"The papers?" The partisan jumped with joy. "Come on, let's go!" He took her by the hand and they started running across the field. In the commotion, he forgot the pail.

"And the water?" she reminded him, even though she was running. But he said, "Later, later. Come on, come on!" And they went down through the pine forest, soon reaching the burned-out house, the base for the formation.

A big, bearded partisan was there on a bench with a machine gun between his knees. He shouted, "O Negro, did you have a kid?"

"The papers, Mazzolino, what are you talking about!"

"Ssss!" commanded the one called Mazzolino. "Keep quiet and leave the ones in the cots alone; they were up all night fighting. We'll read the papers first."

Gelinda distanced herself from them, turned around, undid her strings and her ties, and flattened out the papers with her hands. She was afraid they'd been ruined with her sweat. They were little printed newspapers, small more or less like the protocol papers, and the title was clearly printed, *L'Unità.**

Mazzolino and Negro appropriated the papers, leaned with their backs to the wall, and started to read. Gelinda sat in the shade, waited for a while, and then understood that they wouldn't move easily before the very last line. So she pulled on Negro's jacket.

"I have here two cheeses," she said and she lifted them out of the little shopping bag. "I'm going away now; my mother will be worried. But tell everyone that Gelinda was here, Gelinda the daughter of Big George, the one shot by the Germans."

---

* *L'Unità* is the paper of the Communist party. Founded in 1924 by Gramsci and Togliatti, it is to this day the official organ of the left.

November 1943

The rubble was gray under a gray sky. An entire street, an entire neighborhood, destroyed. The buildings had been tall and full of people. Toward evening the doors opened and closed, families sat down at the table, they stretched out in their beds so that they could get up in the clear and transparent light of a September morning. One of those mornings, so clear and lucid, with the sun shining on the old walls and through small windows, the air force had dropped clusters of incendiary bombs that pierced, penetrated, shattered. The houses folded as if they had been sucked up, four and five floors reduced to a pile of a few meters, and the rest collapsing, caving into the basements. The landscape became a horizon of a few spare walls left standing, still some square footage of rooms painted light blue or pink or green, with some misshapen, random piece of roof balanced on a shattered beam. The street had become a narrow, oblique path running between sad slopes of broken stones, dust, mud, and leftovers here and there, dark and unrecognizable.

Everything was abandoned and deserted, after the screams and sobs and effort with which the dead had been carried away—those who could be, for there were others who were left underneath or who had been so disfigured that it was necessary to just give up. The latter had found their burial in the very moment the bomb had reduced them to nothing, and maybe they had actually suffered less and caused those who searched for them and who had not found them, not seen them, to suffer less. In this way they vanished and were easier to forget.

It was among that gray rubble that Roberto advanced, in the cold of a November day, searching for the ruins of his home. Luckily he had no deaths to cry about. His family had saved themselves hiding in the hills, watching the bombardment with the relief of being far away and knowing they had their best things with them—furniture, utensils, linens. But he, Roberto, knew what he had left down there, hiding in a hole in the wall, and he wanted to attempt the difficult retrieval. Without his fragile mother knowing, crying and fearful as she was, with his indifferent brothers and sisters, Roberto belonged to the Resistance. And now he wanted to find the arms, two revolvers and a musket, hidden with such painful conniving from the unconscious hostility of his family.

He recognized on a wall the old color of the family's kitchen where as a child he had done his homework on the cluttered table while his mother washed dishes, and Marisa and Silvana put make-up on to go to the movies, and Pietro and Carlo pooled their small earnings to buy a ticket for a soccer game. Who knows where he had gotten so much hatred for the Fascists in that squalid, stupid atmosphere. His father had been dead a long time, but he imagined him fighting against the Fascists, due to certain words he had heard old friends say about him, friends who had known him and who regretted having lost him too soon. He remembered a big man who had come to their home one evening, spoken brusquely to Pietro and Carlo, and left saying, "You don't understand who your father was." He had never seen this man again, but that phrase stayed in his mind forever, and only much later did he understand the true meaning. Because of this, Roberto had managed to have a world of his own, a different, constant, and desperate world. And in the end he had managed to get arms, and now he was going to get them, in the heart of the house and the street that had been the scenes of his fervid and confused passion as an adolescent.

Climbing over rocks and bricks, he reached a hollow that corresponded to the stairway. He slipped down the steps toward the basement, and at that point he heard a sound, a cautious step among the ruins. He lifted his head and saw before him a well-known face, Signor Vittorio, a neighbor from the floor above, a Fascist. He was still in his black shirt, under his civilian jacket.

"Ciao, Roberto," said the man, curving over him from above in the half-light of the basement. "What are you doing down there?"

"I came to get something for my mother," he answered. "Something that was left here."

He was immediately sorry about what he'd said, and a shiver passed through his spine. But Signor Vittorio pulled back, disappeared, and Roberto could hear his distant voice, "What a disaster, eh? Good-bye, Roberto!"

He quickly recognized his hiding spot, where he lin-

gered, perplexed, his hands gripping the bag contain-
ing the musket; then he decided against it and buried it
again behind the bricks of the wall. He put only the two
revolvers in his pocket. "That one there is a damned
nuisance, but he can't do anything to me if I leave
empty-handed." But even empty-handed he felt suspect
and vulnerable, and so he took a small ten-liter demi-
john of wine.

On the ruined doorstep he was attacked by the same
voice. "Your mother had hidden the wine, eh?"

"Wine?" Roberto said, looking at the flask. "We need
this for water. Where we're staying there's very little
drinkable water."

Inside him an unvoiced anger was growing, to have
to give so many explanations. But in the pockets of his
jacket under the light raincoat, he felt the hard weight
of the weapons, and he felt stronger knowing that he
had escaped unharmed from the adventure.

"Good-bye, Signor Vittorio," he said, and he started
to walk decisively along the narrow street among the
rocks and dust.

He didn't know if the man was following him; he didn't
dare turn around. He went ahead, looking around the
neighborhood where he had been born, where he had
grown up, where he knew every color of the walls, every
stone in the sidewalk, but which now seemed to him
new and remote, no longer reconstructible from memory, changed forever in the design of its fundamental
lines, a vague horizon, battered, and oscillating like in
dreams. He met a small old woman who was pushing a
cart loaded with things. They greeted each other cor-

dially, like neighbors, but both were too taken with their own efforts to stop and chat. Only now Roberto, when she had passed by, pushing the shafts with effort, found the pretext for looking behind himself, and askance at his Fascist neighbor. And it was then that he saw in the distance, dark and heavy against the dull landscape of the bombed houses, two soldiers of the National Republican Guard. He recognized them as such, peering intently, by their huge gray-green uniforms, and especially by the awkward, large, white pants turned up on the shins. "They are looking for me," he thought in a flash, "and *he* sent them." All of a sudden he threw the flask aside and started to run.

They followed him. Roberto heard the pounding sound of their running against the sound of his own running. It had surely been the Fascist, that spiteful man from upstairs who for so many years he'd seen go out in his black shirt and his fez with the bow. He had informed those two GNRs so that they'd chase him down. They had all the papers they needed to get him because he had been a soldier on September 8.* He had abandoned his company, the regiment, and had escaped, crossing unknown fields until a family of peasants had done something to dress him up in civilian

* From the fall of Mussolini in July 1943 until September 8, forty-five days passed. On this important date, Italy signed a secret armistice with the Allies, in effect withdrawing from the Axis powers but not becoming one of the Allies. Members of the Italian armed forces headed for home, trying to avoid capture and deportation by the German occupiers.

clothes, giving him the possibility of finally returning home. He had barely had the time to get his mother and siblings up into the hills, and to find in a stroke of luck one of his father's old friends, to let him know that he had the arms hidden in a hole in the basement. It had gone too well up to now, everything had gone his way. And now, instead, he was escaping through an unknown and deserted part of town, followed by two military men to whom details and precise orders had been furnished by a well-informed enemy.

In the lightening-sharp sequence of these thoughts, Roberto found his salvation. At the first intersection he turned rapidly, finding a closet that was still standing, and he hurled himself into the dark like a fox. But there, too, he hit against a wall of rubble and had to stop, falling down with a lacerating pain in a swollen ankle. He hoped the soldiers would pass by him as they ran. Instead, they stopped. "He went in here," said a voice, and little by little he saw the outline of the two shadows advance in the foggy light of the entrance. He put his hands in his pocket and took the safety off the pistols. "I'd rather kill them," he thought vaguely, and an immense indolence assaulted him in the same moment, an enormous sense of depression that resembled the fear of no longer being capable of anything.

Maybe the same terror had attacked even the two who had the advantage of strength in numbers, but they also needed to go further in that very dark hole where he, the armed enemy, was hiding. So everyone was completely still, protected and immobile, like in a dead period of a trench war. The long, cold time passed in silence. Roberto, in his little corner among the rocks, almost fell asleep. But all of a sudden he moved abruptly, feeling like a shock the need for action, for movement, for freedom. He couldn't stay there forever with those two guards outside, blocked by a present but unseen force that made it all the more threatening and inexorable. He scraped along the wall with his heart beating loud and painfully against his ribs. He came up next to the pale design of the open door, where he could see the two soldiers at some distance; he heard their voices in a hesitating volley.

With a jump he flung himself out, desperately throwing himself into a run on the resonant stones of the street, and fear lent him an unthinkable speed. He realized that he had gained time and space on those who were following him and that it would be difficult for them to catch him. He turned at a corner and disappeared into an alley. Now he was running free and loose in the miserable, ruined streets, among destroyed houses with empty windows through which you could see the sky, dark in the November dusk. He knew where he was going; certainly not to his family that had taken refuge in the hills, where they were safe. He was headed for another part of the city, a sure and hidden place that seemed like the best solution to his many throbbing perplexities. And it was in that precise moment that a whistle of an air-raid alarm helped him, a tremulous and mournful signal, with a simultaneous slow lighting of a Bengal flare that lit up the unprotected city.

Roberto came running out of the destroyed and deserted neighborhoods, crossing the small, dark streets until he reached the center. And without any fear, he inserted himself in the columns of scared people who were running to reach the shelters. He heard their screams and moans; he left them behind at each basement stair to run farther, happy and light with thoughts as agile as his legs. He touched the weapons in his pockets and repeated in the rhythm of his breath: "I made it, I made it." When the oppressive silence of the wait fell like a curtain on the city, and all that was living seemed still, terrified, and buried, he walked as if he were taking a stroll toward the small house on the outskirts where he knew he would find his predesignated spot. He got there without hurrying, with even breath, so he wouldn't appear to be escaping. He knocked on a well-known door; it opened and he murmured his name in the darkness. He found himself in a warm, well-lit kitchen, in the middle of a circle of jovial and questioning faces. A woman put a bowl of soup on the table for him, and a glass of wine. She told him to eat first, then drink. His father's old friend stood in front of him; when Roberto started to speak, he shook his white head and said, "Eat. We'll talk later."

Roberto felt fine, so fine that two tears of joy fell shining on his hot cheeks. Then the man with the white hair sat down near him and said, "Now tell me everything," as if he were awaiting a long story.

Instead, Roberto spoke in brief sentences, interrupting himself as if the past fear and the present passion burned in him like a fire. "I left the musket there," he said. "I couldn't get it because that Fascist was watching me. It was him; I don't know his name, but he's been our neighbor for many years. He launched the military guards after me; he knew who my father was and that I escaped on the eighth of September. He wanted to get me with the weapons, have me shot or sent to Germany. Or maybe he told the soldiers that I was a scavenger in the rubble. All I could do was run."

He lowered his eyes in shame, hesitating. "I was afraid," he confessed hurriedly, and he stayed there a while in silence.

"But now I know what I have to do," he began again, his voice dry and resolved. "Send me to the mountains with the partisans. Excuse me, but you will not regret having done it."

The old man with the white hair smiled. "Of course we'll send you," he said, and Roberto smiled, too, happily.

"I would like to warn my mother," he added timidly. "So that she's not worried and waiting for me. And I'm sorry about the musket."

"We'll tell your mother," the old man declared. "And we'll get the musket. And maybe even the neighbor."

Death of a Mother

"Good morning, Mamma."

"Good morning, Son."

They greeted each other this way every morning when Professor Ferruccio Levi went to his hospital. His mother almost always watched him from the window as he got into his car and left. Then she went back to the kitchen to discuss lunch with old Maria. They made a contest out of recipes, of specialties, of novelties. "This, this other dish, that's what the professor really likes," they said. But they rarely agreed, especially because the professor, in his quiet, distracted way, ate in haste, praising every food without discriminating.

He never managed to completely disengage his mind from the pediatric clinic he directed. Even in the early afternoon rest hours his thoughts would travel there. He talked about it at length with his mother, using the brutally detached words of a doctor, but with amused sweetness as he told of the children. He remembered them all, one by one, and even his mother knew them through the words of her son. She knew their illnesses, the environment, their condition, and their parents' natures. Often she went to visit them, bringing toys and candy. She entertained herself by guessing their names. "You must be Gino, right? And you're Mario?" and she was almost never wrong.

She had been widowed early, when her son was small. She had loved her husband and had borne a great loss with his death. As a nonpracticing Jew, she didn't believe in a future life. She was sure the dead were lost forever, undone in the earth or in stone. So her child had filled her world; they lived as mother and son, but also as dear friends, as if of the same age. They played together; they studied together. Little by little the boy passed her by, leaving her ever further behind in her limited intelligence. He had left a world of dreams and entered a world of science. He became smarter, more attentive; a doctorate in medicine, and then professor and finally the directorship. He was original and inventive in his cures and discoveries, checking them with the meticulous research of someone who consciously manages human lives. He chose pediatrics because of a pressing inclination toward young, eager existences, and to diminish the suffering of innocents and to correct the blind errors of nature. His work represented an extremely important facet of his life for him. It kept him vigilant and restless, like a sentinel on guard at an unavoidable pass. In all the other acts of his life, he was inexpert, instinctive, timid as a child.

His mother never thought that her son could die. She had never even imagined her own death, except for the vague discomfort of perhaps having to leave him all alone. Their days were placid and unchanging; the years seemed to pass slowly, but indeed they passed quickly. By now the professor was elderly and his mother was ancient, and they had barely noticed. One time Ferruccio came home from the hospital with a terrible cold. He went to bed after taking two aspirin with a small glass of cognac. In the middle of the night he awoke, agitated and hot with fever, and with a cramp at the base of his neck. He felt a strange sensation in the muscles of his legs. The thermometer read one hundred and five; his stomach turned. From one moment to the next, the house became immersed in the strange, peculiar climate of a serious illness, and the consultations and the attempts began. Doctors and professors came and went; they held meetings with serious faces. Ferruccio was no more than the shape of his disease. He looked around himself with empty eyes, groaning with pain as if tortured, turning his head back and forth on the soaked pillow calling his mother but unable to recognize her. He suffered because he didn't see her, but she was there, twenty centimeters from his burning face. "Meningitis," one of the professors said. It was an easy diagnosis, one a doctor barely out of medical school could make. The others were in agreement, also, about the fact that there was no hope of a recovery. The only thing left was to wait for death and announce it to his mother.

They were all amazed at how she behaved, lucid and calm. She stayed by him until his last breath, in silence. She watched him for a day, a night, and then another day on his bed, among the flowers of the coffin. She accompanied him to the cemetery. They expected to see her go mad, from one moment to the next. But she didn't have the strength. She continued to live in silence, as if she, too, had perished.

The years passed. No one knows how the old woman filled her long, empty hours, the slow hours that went from morning to night, and then through the black of night to a new, lost dawn. Toward evening she went to the clinic and sat in the lobby, as she had when the professor was alive. When she entered the white, warm light, she said, "Has the professor left yet?" The doorman greeted her. "Would you like me to call him?" "No, no," she answered, "I'll wait for him." And she sat on the bench, smiling. Now she smiled again at the doorman, at the nurses; she sat a moment, and she left again when no one was looking. She never went to the cemetery, nor did she visit the children.

Sweet and absent as she was, she witnessed the outbreak of war. Still alive in her somewhere was a part that felt compassion for the misfortunes of others, but only superficially, like when a weak wind passes by and ripples the water of a pond, a quick motion that leaves the bottom still and dark. She interested herself in those who were leaving for an unknown and immense front. She comforted their mothers and their wives with brief, light words of hope. And when the bombings started, she refused to abandon the city, or even to go down to the shelter. "You go, Maria, if you think it's right," she said when the siren sounded. And the maid closed the windows and the doors; swearing to herself in her country dialect, she waited for the cloud of noise and fire to pass before finally letting out an angry sigh at the long wail of the cease-fire alarm.

88

Renata Viganò

At a certain moment during the war, even Mrs. Sara Levi née Cremona, eighty years old, alone and shut in her familiar pain, alive only because her organs kept functioning but certainly not by her own will, desire, or pleasure, became a danger for the Nazifascists. A danger to be eliminated. Her name as a Jew belonged on the black lists that in that time were compiled by the Fascists with the help of the census, and then passed along to the Nazis for their collaborative action. And so it was that one morning of an ordinary day, two men from the Black Brigade rang the doorbell of the apartment where Professor Ferruccio Levi, the pediatrician, his name still on the brass plate on the door, had lived. Old Maria came to open the door, thinking it would be the milk boy, and she found before her two dark faces beneath the black berets.

"Signora Levi?" one asked, the ugly, sullen one.

"She is my employer," Maria answered, trying to close the door again. "But she receives no visitors."

"She will receive us," said the other, with a smile that was far from happy. He gave Maria a small push, and the two of them entered.

"She has to come with us," the first one said. "Now."

"Come with you?" Maria exclaimed. "Where? Why? She never goes out."

The two men with the dark faces ignored her. Despite her cries they entered the rooms and took the old woman by the arm. They gave her a vague explanation and made her descend the stairs, mute and stunned. They pushed her into a car. Old Maria ran behind them, shouting. She was barely able to throw the woman's fur coat onto her shoulders in time, as she was then pushed back into the house, threatened with the machine gun. The car left.

And this is how the professor's mother found herself at the station among a crowd of lost people, under a sky of ice. She had no breath to complain; she trembled on her poor, old legs in the middle of a wall of noise, screams, and cries. Someone lifted her up and threw her into a kind of black hole. Her entire body was rigid, filled with cold. She fell on one side, and felt beneath her the confused limbs of other people. A deaf pain penetrated her; she grasped unknown hands and arms. She was pushed aside, sitting against the wall of the wagon. From the window came a gray light, where black shadows passed, bodies and more bodies thrown up in a heap, and so many cries and wails, and the orders of hoarse, lacerating voices. The window closed. For a moment there was relief, darkness, and silence.

To the old woman, squatting in a position that was ill-suited to her hardened joints, it seemed she could barely breathe, as in the pale effort of a dream when you want to walk and you can't, and you suddenly face the horror of a vertical descent without footholds. She hoped to awaken, or at least to move her legs and arms, to lie down on her back, to not feel the tendons strained terribly across every fiber, even the most out-of-the-way and remote ones. But all around her the silence was broken with moans. Others were suffering as she was, tossed by the jumps and jolts of the train car; they were crying even louder. They spoke with desperate and frightened voices, they spoke incomprehensible and inexorable words. The train was moving, and it was dragging them all who knows where. Something out of this world, outside of civilization, beyond life itself. The Nazifascists were deporting people, they were killing millions of human beings. The old woman rested her head on her chest, she unfolded her legs with a great sigh, without noticing that she was knocking against another devastated body. Her last, blinding thought before the darkness was, "How happy I am that you died, Ferruccio!"

Red Flag

Amedea went out into the street, closing the door behind her. From the time she had come back to the city to work as a *staffetta* in the GAP, she was always afraid she might make a mistake. The disastrous incident had left her shaken and sad. She was often overcome by memories, especially the one of the last night down in that miserable countryside the color of winter. The Germans had broken down the door to the house and seized her husband, dragging him away, despite the dangerous and violent resistance he put up, that could neither help him nor come to anything. She ran after them screaming, the group of them banging from side to side, from the furious tugging in one direction and pulling in the other, in his useless effort to free himself. Every time the Germans beat him, new blood dripped from his nose onto his lips, his face already covered with blood. It seemed he would suffocate from the hacking coughs, and the Germans didn't leave him alone a second, not even to let him spit. But he continued to struggle; in any case, he knew that it was a question of life or death.

When the Germans were tired of pulling him forward with pushes and shoves, they gave him an angry kick that made him fall. They jumped on him; one tied his hands behind his back with the belt from his pants, another hauled off and kicked him in the kidneys, the third one took his rifle from his shoulder and let off a burst of gunfire from close range. The body made a sudden, chaotic motion and then relaxed, flat on the ground, in the sparse grass that slowly became bloodied. And she, screaming, covered her eyes but then ran toward those gray, immobile faces with their helmets pulled down over their ears. She beat her fists against the hard cloth of a coat. The German observed her almost with curiosity, and then he laughed.

They went back to where they had come from, the group composed as it had been before, only now they were dragging her. They made her run as they took long soldier steps. She lost her voice, her cries flattened to a deaf sob, which one of the Germans put an end to with two scorching slaps; then he threw her away like a rag in an icy ditch by the side of the path.

"Enough noise" he said. They went away, the three of them, without turning back, and they could no longer hear anything, and that was fine.

She always remembered the taste of being cast aside that the ice had in her mouth that day, when she came to, after who knows how long. She went back near her husband, already black and cold, and she could no longer recognize him. She felt no pain, as if it were not true. "But it is Gino, it's Gino!" she screamed suddenly, desperately, and she ran away disheveled and soaked. She got to the street and found herself among houses, not knowing how she'd gotten there, in the arms of frantic people who held her. And her cries began again;

everyone in the village heard them and shook with grief. Later, in the dark, the relatives were allowed to go get the dead man with a stretcher. They washed him and arranged the body for burial. Only when she saw him on the bed did Amedea realize that she had so many tears still to shed.

And from that point on, as soon as she got back to the city, she joined the GAP. Although she'd been so afraid of the bombings at first, now they meant nothing to her. And nothing else scared her either, except the thought that some imprudent action or error on her part might put her comrades in danger. She was the cook at the camp, she had learned to clean the guns, she washed and ironed. She went out whenever and wherever they sent her, and she was happy only when a mission was done. On her own, she kept herself busy gathering foodstuffs, either with her own rations or on the black market. There was never enough for the hungry boys of the partisan brigade.

"The tenth of June," she thought. "It's been four years that this war has been going on. Already seven months since they killed Gino." She looked to the left and the right, there was almost no one around. It was a beautiful evening; it was warm. She crossed the street to enter the butcher's, taking out the ration cards from her purse. While she was waiting her turn, she saw in the mirror of the shop that behind her a man had entered. She met his gaze, the stare of those two eyes. Her heart started to beat hard; she tried to stop it by controlling her breathing, but she was afraid it was beating in the veins in her neck.

"Three rations of boiled meat, please," she said when it was her turn, and she put the ration cards on the counter. "And a little more, if it's possible."

"It's impossible," the butcher answered. He, too, was on alert, since an unknown man was in the shop. "And you, sir?" he added, trying to free himself of the terror.

"Nothing, thanks," he said brusquely. He turned and left.

Amedea pretended nothing was happening. She paid without hurrying. She saw the strange individual had stopped in front of her house. So she changed her normal route, reaching home only after a long meandering, crossing deserts of leftovers from the bombings. She entered by the back entrance. There was only big Charlie, snoring in his cot. She shook him.

"There's someone watching us," she said, short of breath. They peeked from behind the closed shutters. They didn't see him, but there were two others now who stood immobile on the sidewalk in front of the house.

"Damn," Charlie swore, "our goose is cooked. Get the guns and the ration cards out of here. I'll try to warn the comrades."

They put three pistols and the rest in a bag.

"What will you cover them with?" Charlie asked.

"I'll take care of it," Amedea said with a sudden idea. She looked behind the bathroom tub for some underwear that she had hidden there, special articles she needed to wear for a "common ailment." She arranged them in the bag and then covered them with a newspaper.

"I'm ready," she said. "This is fine." And she went down the stairs right away, embarrassed that maybe Charlie would see. But when she stuck her head out to see the landscape of rubble behind the house, there he was, that guy, leaning against a column that had been left standing. He was waiting for her and obviously knew about the second entrance. "Halt! The police!" he said. She had to stop.

"Put your bag down," he ordered. "What do you have there?"

"My things, some dirty laundry," Amedea answered. She showed him without shame. She thought maybe Charlie was on his way down; she recognized his quick step. And there he was; he grabbed the soiled sanitary napkin from her hand.

"Red flag," he said and then delivered a calm, robust, and solemn fist to the policeman, a blow that knocked him to the ground. You could hear the sound of his head hitting the cobblestones.

"Damn," said Charlie. "Give me a pistol, Amedea, and run."

The Viaduct

He often said, "I could have stayed in Bologna, at the university. I would have done my little thesis, gotten a degree in Engineering. A nice little thesis!" And then he'd show his laughing, sickly face that wouldn't tan like the others in the mountain sun. "The problem was that you had to go to school in a black shirt, and it wasn't flattering to my complexion!" He winked, and then he seemed very young. In the brigade, his battle name was Little Thesis.

They were camped up there, in a village without a street that was called La Cantoria,* maybe because there was a kind of demolished ruin that vaguely resembled a chapel. Only one family was left living near the partisans, in the little house that was deepest in the valley. They were courageous and reliable people—the father, the mother, and the two girls, two mature, beautiful girls who worked like men. One of the sons had died in Greece, and the other's whereabouts were unknown. "Certainly, he's not with the Fascists, nor with the Germans, our Primo, even if . . . ," the head of the household, Valente, would say. And he'd stop at that *even if,* full of anguish, when he'd see his wife, Gigia's glance.

* The word means "choir stall."

It was always Little Thesis who would comfort him. "Keep your chin up, big daddy. Primo will come back; he's like us, he's with the partisans. He'll come back when we've already gone!" He made his usual face, a bit mischievous and surprised. He called Valente "daddy" and "big daddy," but he never called Gigia "mamma Gigia" like all the others. One evening, when he really wanted to let himself go—maybe he just couldn't take it anymore, keeping quiet in the middle of all those people who spoke so little—he even explained why. He had never known his own father; he hadn't existed practically. And his own last name was that of his mother. But his mother, all alone, had been marvelous.

"I had everything, even more than the other children. And she always worked, my mother. She was a seamstress, and I was the little lord. Even as a teenager, even as a student. This is why I want to become an engineer. And one day my mother will be a lady, it will be her turn. And even if I love Gigia dearly, I cannot call her 'mamma.'" He turned around, as if to ask forgiveness, but Gigia was laughing with her blue eyes in the folds of her wrinkles. And Fosca and Tita, the girls, said "Yes, yes," because, in effect, they couldn't have cared less. And the boys in the brigade were a bit amused and a little annoyed at so much mawkishness. Especially Big Hugh, who grumbled one evening, saying he didn't like stories about little lords, and as for a mamma at home, well, he had one too, and so did the others, and chattering about it was a waste of time and softened the heart.

"You mean you go weak just remembering home?"

the commander, Sarno, observed. He was the type who always wanted to get to the bottom of things.

"No," Big Hugh answered. "But look, since I decided to come up in the mountains, I don't like chatter, good or bad that it may be, and not even among ourselves. Actions are what keep us warm, not words."

"Okay," said Sarno, with that sour tobacco voice, a voice that came from cigarettes or, in the absence of those, the cigarettes made from dried grasses. "Let's not go overboard. It's better to talk amongst ourselves during those hours when we've got nothing to do. Otherwise we don't get to know each other, and in battle it's as if we're thrown together by chance. Many things can go wrong exactly because you feel like strangers, even if we're of the same idea, or from the same town."

"You know more about it than I," Big Hugh concluded. "I'm quick to forget how ignorant I am."

He shook his big, obstinate head and was surprised when the commander put an arm around his neck and hugged him with unexpected warmth. Small as the commander was, he barely reached Big Hugh, whose stature rendered displays of affection awkward and very rare.

Autumn stripped the thin shrubs of the plateau, which had no woods or fields but only nude slopes with landslides and gullies. The wind was cold and carried the color of winter. "It will soon snow," Valente said, and he hurried to bring the cow and the sheep out to pasture to save the little fodder he had in the barn. The partisans were discussing if it might not be better to change location.

"We're not doing anything here," Sarno said. "The streets are far away. If the bad weather blocks us, we'll find ourselves wintering here like refugees. The Germans will never come over the ridge, unless they attack in force and we'll have to decamp and beat it. We chose a lousy place."

"Aside from the fact," Big Eater observed—he was a strong boy, though always hungry—"that we can't count on this family's provisions, and we don't have enough to eat here . . ."

"Let's go," the commander cut in. "We'll send a *staffetta* over to the guys in Cimazzo. We'll join their formation that's always on the attack at the junctions. There's plenty to do down there, against the German back-ups . . ."

In the gelid space of the big room, around the glowing coals of the fire, the waiting boys moved about with joy. They were tired of hiding there, inert, on that arid, rocky plain, where the only thing they fought was the wind.

"But wait a second," a weak, questioning voice suddenly sounded. Everyone turned around. It was Little Thesis. "Wait a second," he repeated, coming forward. "We didn't think of the viaduct."

"The viaduct?" Sarno asked, and since the others were murmuring, he shouted "Silence!"

"It's not right here," Little Thesis explained, and the

dark and red reflections from the fire passed across his face. "Yesterday I walked four hours to it, two going and two coming." He smiled with the happiness of a child.

"It's beautiful," he continued. "It runs along the back road against the side of the mountain. An admirable job, all the transverse pylons set into the rock and not the crumbly earth. If you could knock it down, the German traffic would be interrupted. And good-bye— no more passing through that way!"

"It's an idea," the commander said. "We can stay here a little while longer."

They talked about it for a long time, around the dying embers. No one felt the cold anymore, and even Big Hugh, the slowest of them all, was lively and enthusiastic, maybe even a bit intoxicated, as if he'd drunk a good bottle of wine. The evening hours passed in a flash. Later, everyone was asleep except the two guards, panting and quivering, waiting for the change.

The snow began to fall as if it, too, were curious to see what was about to happen. Down down down, like a cloth quilt pulled down from a roll, on a stage.

"Just looking at it hurts the eyes!" Little Thesis said.

"It all hurts," said Big Hugh, upset as if the weather were offending him personally. They marched off to Valente's house around noon, Sarno and seven men, among whom were Big Hugh and Big Eater. The other five stayed behind.

"Don't throw a tantrum, Little Thesis," Sarno warned in his effective way, a dark look with gentle words. "But Tita is going to guide us to find the place."

He watched them leave, a short line of black figures with their feet sinking into the snow. At the last moment he couldn't even distinguish which one was Tita. "Huh!" he said painfully. "Tita is only a girl."

He had such a small, funny face in that moment that even Gigia started to laugh. Then each person took his place, either working or waiting, passing drop by drop those hours that were always the most tiring and the worst. While she was giving him his bowl of soup, Fosca murmured to Little Thesis, "We're very familiar with the viaduct, we and all the girls in this area. We used to go there with our boyfriends!"

They looked up at the white sky; the snow had eaten the trail, and the slow wave fell, light and gray. It seemed almost impossible that they were speaking of boyfriends under the arches of the viaduct in a season filled with broom and elderberry and with the sun on the grass. Three partisans and Valente were playing cards. Gigia was at the fire with her few pans.

"Let's you and I go outside and guard, Little Thesis," Fosca said loudly, so that everyone could hear. Maybe she wanted to console him, or maybe she didn't want to feel inferior to her sister.

"We'll hear the explosion better, too," Little Thesis answered. He ran behind her, tightly wrapped in a coat that was too light for the season, through the crunching snow.

There was no explosion. Sarno came back with his men, and he brought inside a faint odor of frost and a cloud of breath. They were all red or blue and they took their shoes and coats off noisily. You could see in their

shapeless movements the anger of the unsuccessful maneuver. They went off to their ruined chapel after having melted the cold from their joints as best they could,
and they threw themselves down on the straw and blankets. No one wanted to speak.

Sarno brought those who had not taken part up to
date: "We found the place with no trouble, even if we
did have snow up to our knees. That girl is terrific. As
we put the detonator together, we thought we could
then dive for cover up the side of the mountain, where
we went the other day to bring the explosives. This time
the snow was so high we had to lengthen the fuse to
give ourselves time to escape, at least by the road, and
get ourselves a safe distance away. But the long fuse got
wet and went out. Damn it all . . ."

"Maybe I could come the next time," said the meek
voice of Little Thesis.

"I don't know if there'll be another time," answered
Sarno. "Quiet now, and try to keep warm. I can't talk
any more about it."

By now, however, the viaduct was in the thoughts of
every partisan, like a necessity. They constantly talked
about it, even without naming it. They called it "down
there" in their discussions. Winter had spread along the
mountainside with piles of snow and windstorms. But at
the Cantoria and in Valente's house they thought only
about "down there," like believers think about heaven.
"Down there," the Germans and the Fascists went along
with their loaded vehicles; it was a bottleneck, a fold
made of curved arches. Among the partisans each one
had his say. Taken all together, the only thing left to do

was blow up the viaduct. Even Big Hugh admitted that this time "chatting" had served a purpose.

They marched again one day when it was just starting to rain. The ice was melting into water that soaked the skin, and their steps sunk into the wetness without the protection of the snow. They were all worried about the explosives that, while protected, could absorb some of the humidity that would dissolve their power. Little Thesis went with Fosca to the end of the line, and he smiled at times for no reason. Even his timid face had tanned with the crude reflection of the snow. It seemed he was very happy. When they got "down there," they scattered throughout the holes and arches of the viaduct; they were finally where they had wanted to be for so long. Hours and hours of hard work. The German trucks clattered by, their drivers calm on that isolated street. And the partisans would have to stop and hide, even if darkness was on their side. One beam from a headlight would be enough to set off a disaster. But nothing happened and they returned, walking along among the puddles. The fuses were long, but in a dry place. They couldn't miss this time.

They heard the impressive explosion from far away and shouted with joy in the desertedness of the mountain. They hugged each other, but not too tight in their soaking clothes, and then returned home to the Cantoria to warm themselves with the little fire and little food.

Little Thesis turned his warm, childlike face around to his companions: "I did my degree on the viaduct."

Argelide

"Argelide!" called old Marina, coming around the corner of the house. "Do you need anything? Secondo and I want to go to bed."

Argelide was seated on the stone bench facing the golden sunset on the plains. She turned gently and answered, "No, nothing. Thanks, Marina. Good night."

She liked to be alone in that silent, colorful hour. She looked at the old landscape, forgotten in so many years of being away, and she recognized it little by little: rows of vines and hedges, the fields and silhouettes of the houses, the same as when she was a young girl. But then she had grown tired of it, seeing it always the same, solitary and deserted, varying only in the monotonous change of the seasons. For every person there was a corresponding heavy task involving arms, back, legs, and a reaction of chills or sweat. As soon as the cycle was complete, it began again. "I don't want to be a peasant," Argelide had decided one day.

Her father died from an illness he had lived with for three years, brought on by a ferocious beating from the Fascists. Who knows how they had hit him that cold-blooded night, with their hard wooden clubs! He was strong as an ox, but he never got back his great, peaceful health. He kept his hands on his still-aching stomach, ate little, and started to lose weight. Argelide remembered how she and her mother had cried and almost wished for his death, because to see him suffer so was unbearable. Then they felt sorry and were sick with remorse. Argelide trembled when she remembered those days. Her mother had grieved so much, she lost herself in a benign fog of oblivion. "Now I really won't have to be a peasant," Argelide told herself with immense bitterness, when she was forced to accompany her mother to the psychiatric hospital.

She sold the farmland and closed up the house, leaving two rooms to the old tenants Marina and Secondo without asking for rent, and she left for the city. A few months later people in the village said she'd been spotted in the center of town, well dressed and made up; she was walking along quickly, looking healthy, blond, triumphant. And if she met someone from the village, she turned her eyes away and didn't say hello to anyone.

Now, with the war, she had returned to the house, full of darkness and her childhood, and it made her both happy and melancholy. In her wayward life, one fixed point had remained, a place where she could head for, where she could rest, like a prosperous retired person, when she no longer had any desire to keep busy. Years earlier she had had the little property fixed up, and now it seemed more of a villa than a country home; but even though she was proud of it as if it were some kind of victory, she had never bothered to live there. She still preferred the apartment in the city, even if she often felt it oppressed her, a pale solitude in those frequented but closed rooms. The traces of her country-girl origins showed in her desire for wide horizons and a free and open sky, and she suffered without realizing it, vaguely discontent and misty, even if the humble events of her empty existence proceeded in a relatively happy way.

The return to the village, for now, had not been favorable. Her long absence and unclear reputation had earned her jealousy and suspicion that came together in a moralistic severity based on a fragile construction of sudden intolerance.

"How strange!" Argelide thought, sitting next to her door as the night opened with a large, white, brazen moon. "I escaped a bombing that destroyed the enormous shelter of the Savings Bank. They said it was completely safe and bomb-proof. Instead, a cluster of bombs fell and caved in the floor. I was in a little corridor and could get out only after several hours. My mouth, my eyes, my hair were completely filled with dust when they pulled me out." She touched her head with her open hands. "My hair stayed that way, dry and coarse—maybe it will never go back to being as it was before." After that huge scare, her mind continued to retrace the memory, and she felt she would never again think of anything else.

But now the hostility of her hometown was a new source of unpleasant sensations, and she got more anger from it than regret. "I've never done anything bad to these people," she reflected, immersed in a sweet, humid silence torn only by the chirping of the crickets. "Did I take their husbands, their friends, their boyfriends? I didn't even want to see them, can you imagine, especially because of the dirty tongues around here. The ones I knew were completely different, they made me a lady. And now I can stay here in peace, far away from the bombs."

She fell again into the abyss of that moment when she saw the shelter disintegrate. "There were two old ladies, so nice. They were really respectable, two virgin old maids. They didn't talk to me, but they always said hello. They said something to me while we were running down the stairs, and I answered that there was nothing to fear, the shelter was strong. Instead they stopped in the bigger room; they were squeezed in there with so many others. The bombs destroyed everything; they exploded in the crowd. They all ended up in pieces. Even the two old maids, nothing was found of them, and there wasn't even a funeral . . ." She could see the two delicate faces crushed and wrinkled like old photographs, their innocent smiles that forgave without trying to justify her. And she heard again her father's constricted moaning, his immense suffering, here in this very same house, where her mother had said, "It's better that he has died . . . It's better, it's better . . ." She felt sorry for herself, for her young life, so worn out, battered, and stale. A sense of loss gnawed at her stomach, creating an emptiness. She started to cry hot and copious tears that shone on her cheeks in the light of the moon.

Someone with a cautious, quick step came through the open gate from the street. Argelide dried her eyes and ran into the shade of the little drive.

"Who is it?" she said, trying to keep her voice steady.

"Delfino," the other voice answered. "Good evening, Argelide."

It was a boy from her past, now become a man. They hadn't seen each other in years; maybe in a different place they wouldn't even have recognized each other. He was massive, sturdy, sure of himself; she had gained weight with her wide, flat face white from staying away from the sun.

"You came back. Will you stay long?" Delfino asked.

"Maybe. I don't know," Argelide said uncertainly. "I got stuck in a bombing. My house was destroyed."

"I'm glad you're back," Delfino hinted under his breath.

They stood in front of each other, looking hesitantly. Both of them had so much to say, and Argelide went first. "If it's true, then you're the only one in town. The others would have preferred that I not return!" Breathing heavily as she got worked up, she harshly let out her secret rancor. She added, "In town they held me in high regard. Very respectable people were my friends, two wealthy ladies from a very good family, for example, lived on my street, and they both died in the bombing, poor things. And I didn't go by the name Argelide, you know, but Jenny, Miss Jenny . . ." She spoke rapidly, as if imploring him to believe her. "Here, on the other hand, they look at me in such a way . . . This morning I met the schoolteacher, Gina, that Fascist, in her uniform with her beret. It would have made the rocks laugh. She passed right by me with her two daughters, two wrinkled monkeys looking for husbands. You should have seen the looks! And not just them—the tobacconist, and Giulia from the inn, and Costantina at the post office, and other stupid, ill-mannered people. 'Oh, Argelide, how are you doing, Argelide is life treating you well, Argelide . . .'" She stopped, out of breath and once again near tears.

"Don't take it so hard," said Delfino, and he put one of his huge hands on her shoulder. "Come here with me, let's sit a while."

They sat near each other on the stone bench. He pulled a pack of cigarettes out of his pocket and they smoked in silence. From the countryside, reinforcing the sound of the crickets, came a distant chorus of frogs.

"How nice it is here," Argelide said quietly.

"Indeed," Delfino began. "That's why I'm here and why I want to speak to you. Let me talk; answer me only after I've finished—in the meantime I promise you that you'll end up liking it here, despite the imbeciles, because this is your village and you are at home here. I remember your father and your mother, and I can trust you. And I'm not the only one who thinks like this, but many other comrades and friends who know how you've suffered in your family . . ." He interrupted himself and lit another cigarette, and she stayed very still and quiet, almost holding her breath. ". . . at the hands of those damned Fascists, who brought so much ruin on us all. And now there's the Germans, and you know we're going to have to put up with all sorts of things . . . We may even lose our lives. So we thought it was stupid to sit here and wait for them to kill us without doing anything, and we got together, all the good ones, in the organization. You must know that there are partisans fighting to get rid of the Fascists and Germans as soon as possible, and trying to save what's left to save, bloody hell! And have those Allies come forward once and for all, that up 'til now all they've done is drop bombs! . . ." He swore through his teeth, and threw away the cigarette.

In the meantime, Argelide moved and said, "Really. You're really right."

"I'm going on," Delfino continued, but now he seemed less certain, and sought the words with care. "I have to tell you that when you were away, we came here sometimes for our meetings. It's an isolated house. The Nazifascists don't come around here at night. They're afraid."

This time he looked Argelide in the face, decisively, and he asked, "Are you angry that we came?"

She was surprised, attentive, and shook her head no; she wanted to say something, but Delfino didn't give her time. "They were in agreement, Secondo and Marina. We hid some draft dodgers here. They were in danger of being shot . . . But then you came . . ." Again he stopped her from speaking with a gesture. "And now, listen to me, and I'll tell you everything: we thought we could come, you know, one at a time, up here to your place. Don't get upset, excuse me. Since in the village they consider you . . . As you told me earlier, no one would suspect anything. We'll be friends that come to see you, get it? And sometimes we may even have a little party together, with someone playing the

accordion . . . In the meantime there would be someone . . . We could have the meeting, you see? You'd be
helping us a lot, Argelide, think about it."

He took a deep breath and wiped his brow. He was
sweating.

"So," Argelide began very slowly, "I should start,
here, too . . ."

"Not really, not if you don't want to," Delfino murmured. "It's only an act, a cover . . ." He felt indiscreet
and out of place and didn't dare look her in the face.

"But in town they'll believe it," Argelide said.

"So, what do you care?" exclaimed Delfino, and concluded, "Didn't you already say that they don't say hello
to you? This would be the best answer to that!"

She brushed the back of one hand slowly against the
palm of the other. Many moments of her life passed
through her mind, the many men who had passed by
without stopping. She saw her father reduced to a cadaver, her mother in the lunatic asylum. The old ladies
in the shelter. The dead on the stretchers. She thought
again about the teacher, Gina, with her ugly daughters
and the Fascist uniform.

"OK," she said suddenly. "I'll do everything you tell
me to."

So in the days that were almost white with the great,
summer heat and in the sweet evenings and the dusks
just before the curfew, visitors started arriving at Jenny's
house. Some came along the road that runs by the river,
others from the town. The door was always closed and
didn't open easily. In the back of the house, Secondo

and Marina kept watch. The fast tongues of the piazza sewed the pieces together, and no one intervened to make them stop. The Germans had other diversions and the fact didn't interest them. For the Fascists, the place was too far away and lonely; it wasn't to their taste.

Jenny was never in plain view. She was pent up like a prisoner. If it hadn't been for the wide horizon and the trees and the fresh breath of the river, she would have thought she was in her dark rooms in the city. But inside, her life had become intense and rich, full of unknown thoughts and things both horrible and marvelous. She wasn't upset that people talked about her. And she didn't care if they called her Jenny.

Everything ended one morning when Delfino came running up to tell her that the Germans and the Fascists had spied on them. Now they had to abandon their base; it had already been burned.

"We're all going away," he said. "They may do a round-up. The others have already been warned. You escape, too, I'm warning you. Go with Marina and Secondo. They'll know where to take shelter." He gave her a quick caress on her ruined, withered hair, and disappeared among the trees in the direction of the river.

"Good-bye," said Argelide.

She decided not to go with Marina and Secondo, and they were so scared that they didn't put up a fight. She put a few things in a bag and dug out the bicycle that had once again been buried in the barn. They said good-bye quickly and almost without tears, in the haste and the anguish. She found herself alone, pedaling along the street full of heat and dust. Only then did she start to cry, and with her white and crying face, the new bicycle, and her good dress, she became an unusual figure that day on that street. Unusual—and suspect. They took her at the city gates; she could not explain where she was coming from nor where she was going. The Fascists kept her in their barracks one night. A few wanted to have a good time with her; they tied her up to keep her still. The morning after they didn't know what to do with her. They put her on a train of deportees that was leaving for Germany.

Thin Walls

The two soldiers in black shirts dragged the hand-cuffed boy along the corridor; one of them opened a door with a big key that was hanging from the bunch. And he said, "Throw him in here, this shit. He'll be with a colleague. Take the cuffs off. And you, take this," and he unloaded a forceful backhand on the boy's mouth, while the other soldier slipped the handcuffs off. Then they gave him a push, and he fell forward into the darkness, painfully hitting a shoulder against a sharp edge of something. He grabbed onto it and managed to hold himself up on his knees, his lips sealed and without complaining. The door closed behind him.

The entire house shook, pierced by the cries and blows. The soldiers of the Republican National Guard brought the citizens who had been rounded up and distributed bread to them on the floors of the "barracks." You could hear someone crying hard, with a high-pitched and convulsive shriek. They were certainly beating him, and the hollow sound of the blows resounded in the cry. He was finally silent when they slammed him behind a door with a loud thud, after a burst of obscenities. You could still hear strained cries, persistent, petulant cries, and finally a sole voice, clearly: "Enough!

Finish it off!" Authoritative steps echoed along the corridor, in the midst of a sudden calm. Maybe it was the commander. Indeed, the same tenor voice began again, "And make especially sure nothing can be heard outside, you hear? We are not in a barracks, right? This is a villa in the suburbs, thin walls . . ."

The words were lost in a faraway echo of empty rooms. A shuffling, some murmuring, other confused noises. Then the silence again.

"Who's there?" asked a voice in the small room, from someone stretched out on the cot. The boy was still there as he had fallen, leaning against the wall. He had extended his legs, and he slowly massaged his hurt shoulder. Even his mouth burned, and he labored to move it to speak.

"My name is Piero Santi, and you? They said you're one of my colleagues . . ."

The man on the cot laughed shortly. "A colleague in misfortune," he said. "Do you have a match? I have a bit of candle. They keep us in the dark here, even during the day."

The boy rummaged in his pockets quickly. "I don't have matches," he whispered, and he felt like he was announcing an immense disaster. "They took them away with the cigarettes."

The other let out a great sigh. "I've been in here since Saturday, all locked up. And today is Tuesday. They gave me a lit candle the first evening: as long as it lasts, they said, and then, good night. So I put it out almost right away, to save it. When they bring me my food, a little light comes in through the door. There's another cot—if you feel around, you'll find it. This way you can stretch out and rest. We'll talk in the dark."

Piero got to his feet, rowing with his outstretched hands. He found a military blanket at his fingertips and lay down as if he were defeated. In that moment he felt he'd fallen into a warm well-being, and he hoped to fall asleep. He no longer wanted anything, not even to feel alive. He closed his eyes in the black pitch that was on top of him like a wall, but he immediately felt his breath come with difficulty, anxiously, and he jumped up again, oppressed and afraid.

"There's very little oxygen," said the voice from the other cot. "Because of the smell, too. You know, unfortunately, there's a kind of garbage can, a disgusting thing. I tried to cover it with my shirt, but you can still smell it. But you get used to breathing slowly and moving carefully. Try to stay calm, Piero."

A note in that voice revealed in a flash a world of things that were well-known and had been suffered. Piero could see himself in the middle of his deep, clear, detached memory: a country road in the rain. That same voice had called "Maria Chiara," and Maria Chiara took him arm-in-arm, leaning toward him. Meanwhile he, Piero, hidden by the brush in the vegetable garden, was watching. Maria Chiara came running along in the puddles with her wet shoes, her black hair soaked and sparkling with drops. She was meeting Michele Ferriti, the rich man, the *signore*. Michele Ferriti, a fat, young man, slow, always red in the face, not handsome, not elegant. And yet Maria Chiara walked arm-in-arm with him, she leaned toward him, she was slightly taller, and she kissed him lightly on the balding forehead. And they went away together laughing, right on that country road and in front of that vegetable garden. Now Piero knew that his colleague on the cot was the same man who had taken his girlfriend away.

"The worst thing is," Michele said with the dignified shame of one who has always had a decent bathroom in the house, "the bodily needs. Well, you see, ..."

"No, no, no!" Piero suddenly screamed, leaping toward the door. "No. I cannot stay closed up in here," and he started to bang furiously with his fists on the wood. "Open up, open up, help!" He backed up groping along, tripping over the cots; he hit against the bars of the shutters at the window. "Help! Help! You're free to make it, if you can. Suit yourself! Feel free! Not me. I'll scream, scream, screeeeeeam!"

In the corridor rose a roar of steps, the key turned in the lock, the door opened. In the pale light appeared a black figure. Piero lurched forward, finding himself against the round hole of a rifle.

"You're crazy," the soldier announced angrily. "Get on the cot, idiot, or I'll kill you."

"In the dark no, in the dark no!" Piero shouted desperately, but he felt himself taken by the shoulders and thrown down forcefully onto the rough blanket.

"Stupid idiot," Michele whispered in his ear, a warm and panting murmur. "Do you want them to kill us?"

"In the dark no," Piero yelled again, in the grasp of the big hands, kicking like one possessed. Michele threw himself on top of him, suffocating the cries with a fist pressed against his mouth. He managed to keep him immobile at all costs, without worrying if he was hurting him or not. And right in that moment another new voice, a foreign voice, exploded in the tumult. "Why here dark?" the voice said. "Light!"

The soldier had the nailed planks broken apart, flinging open the windows and the shutters. Beyond the grille was the warm light of the sunset. Everyone looked at each other for a second, batting their eyelashes.

The German noncommissioned officer had entered and was standing there, his legs spread apart, thin, straight, anonymous. He looked like an infinite number of other German rank officers like himself, as if they'd all been cut from a mold. He looked at the small room with colorless eyes from the ceiling to the floor, the two disordered bunks, the garbage in the corner, a broken stool, and a pile of straw and old rags. He pulled his nose up and sniffing the air, he headed toward the Fascist soldier. His face was absolutely inexpressive and yet threatening as he said, "Here no good. You no do duty!" He blocked the answer with his high, strident voice. "You follow orders. And enough!"

The black shirt open on the man's neck was trembling, as were his hands on the rifle. The German barely touched his arm with a rigid, outstretched finger. "Clean," he intimated. "We great army. No dirty." With the same despising finger he skimmed the points of the collar. "And you close shirt."

He turned his back and left. In the corridor, two other rapid shadows passed and they heard some muffled words. For a moment, a light laugh rose, sharp, a woman's laugh, but it was covered by the sound of a motor starting. Two mute, dark-faced orderlies came to do a superficial cleaning, and they took the garbage can away. Before closing the door one said, "Make your beds, and don't go looking for trouble. The guard is outside." He opened the door again a crack and added, "For the bathroom, just knock."

Michele and Piero sat in silence, breathing with their faces to the grille. The sky was luminous and gray, and the scent of the air was good. But there were still so many hostile and difficult things between them, and surrounding them the uncertainty, the precariousness of life.

"Why did you take my girlfriend?" Piero exclaimed, as if there were nothing more important.

"I took your girlfriend?" Michele asked. "No, maybe I saved you from death. She was there, before, our Maria Chiara. Didn't you recognize the voice? Now she's with the Germans and she makes them call her Claretta."*

Later, during the night when they were calm and stretched out on the cots, Michele began to explain. "You ran into trouble with the round-up because you were among those who opposed the threshing, right? For me, though, it's a completely different deal. I can tell you, because 'they' already know about it. I was directing the partisan organization here. I made a mistake, I admit it, making love with Maria Chiara, but it

* The name is an ironic reference to Claretta Petacci, Mussolini's mistress.

seemed like she was with us, an anti-Fascist, enthusiastic. I trusted her. The problem came when her father, the great Barnaba Bruno, the biggest café–pastry shop–drugstore owner of the city, was nominated secretary of the Fascist headquarters, in place of the other one they'd killed. I told Maria Chiara that we could never see each other again. She already knew a lot about me, she'd been helping me up 'til then, secretly. She threw herself on my neck; she didn't want to let me go. She swore she would give me precious information; what's more, she told me it was lucky her father was in that group . . ."

Michele paused here, and it was a painful pause. "Who knows if at least in that one moment she was sincere. Or maybe she was just reciting her part. I would like to believe that she wasn't such a shit from the beginning, that maybe they forced her, blackmailed her later. In any case, I," his voice got louder, in a bitter, lacerated sound, "was an idiot."

Piero was silent on his prickly blanket. He tried to imagine how the red, puffy face must have been after those words. An astonishment was growing in him that was almost a disbelief: Michele Ferriti, the rich man, the *signore,* was a man of action, a partisan who risked his life. He never would have thought such a thing, and instead it was the truth, proven by deeds.

"She turned me in, surely," said Michele. "Everyone knew that I was supposed to be out of town that night. Only she reached me a few minutes before and gave me terrible news. The Fascists were surely going that night to take our men at one of our bases. She didn't know which one, but I had to believe her. On the chance it was true, I had to warn the comrades. I left on my bicycle, and they stopped me after fifty meters, on the street of my own house. It wasn't true—they didn't know where the base was. It was a trick to take me away in secret, to throw me in here. I'll repeat it: I was an idiot."

"And now?" Piero asked, anxiously, feverishly.

"Nothing," Michele answered. "They didn't do anything to me except keep me here, confined in the dark. To weaken me. And I'm sure they're preparing an interrogation . . ." His voice faltered for a moment, but then returned, controlled and strong. "I'm sorry for my parents. But remember: whatever happens, I'm not giving anybody up. Whatever they do to me, remember: I don't know anything, I'm not saying anything. I want you to know it. And now, sleep. We have to sleep, we're too tired."

"Good night," Piero whispered, with a heavy voice like a child who has cried. He extended his hand, it met Michele's and grasped it. It was cold, remote, pathetic. In a silent alternation of sleep and waking, they waited together for the sun to rise on a false dawn.

All day long Piero waited for Michele to be brought back. They had taken him away as he was, in pants and a shirt, together with others. You could hear the racket in the hallway, the voices of the German rank officer and the Fascist commander, the noise of a truck. Then nothing, for hours and hours. The window was open on a wooded field, with an orchard in the distance. Piero stayed with his face in the sun, and he felt freer, immersed in the summer day like a fish in water. Anxiety milked the sweat from him in drops that fell slowly down his cheeks, pushed along by the tears. He almost didn't realize he was crying. He was thinking vague, unconnected thoughts. From time to time, he threw himself on the cot, but then got up again right away, afraid of falling asleep there, alone and not knowing how he would wake up, or even if he would wake up. At noon the soldier came and brought him a mess-tin of soup and some bread. He had asked for wine and some cigarettes, paying with the last five-hundred bill that he had left, jammed down into his jacket pocket. "I'll bring you the change," the soldier had said. But he'd not seen him again, and when Piero knocked for the toilet, another soldier came to accompany him.

The "barracks" seemed deserted: there was the odor of disinfectant, of mold, of wet cloth, and the great warmth of the June sun. A shining melancholy invaded the hallway, the half-open, empty rooms. But from the inside, or on the floors above, Piero perceived a buzz, a murmuring, some exclamations, some knocking. The house contained a mass of fear, pain, wickedness, unconsciousness, and it tended this in the middle of its field and its orchard. It was a beautiful, sad house, one with walls that were too thin. With a shiver, Piero understood why they had taken Michele and the others away, and in what state they must be now. He imagined the wide face that he had hated and that now he loved. Before, it was red with wealth and health, and now it was white for all the blood they had uselessly taken out of it. In that moment, he heard the sound of the cars and he ran toward the door that was opening.

"Go, get out of here, go home!" the soldiers said, pushing a pile of dazed and trembling men.

"Go, go, you too," said the one who had taken the five hundred lire without giving him the change.

There was even the German rank officer, very excited. "Out, out! *Raus!*"

Piero found himself, reeling from a push, on the asphalt drive in front of the gate. He saw the girl, standing not far away. Maria Chiara Bruno, but no longer her, the one he had known, the one he had danced with and kissed for long hours in the night, in the countryside. She appeared ugly, arrogant, and brazen, too thin in her safari jacket and rather ridiculous with her tilted beret and riding crop. He ran away with his head down, he was so tempted to haul off and give her a slap. He murmured to himself confusedly as he escaped, "Poor Michele, thank you, forgive me. I know what you wanted to tell me. That bitch won't be having anyone else killed. I swear to you, Michele."

He Knew German

He was a common man, like so many others. Pino brought him into the brigade one cold, foggy evening, almost dragging him along on the mule path so that he didn't fall down into the ravine. In the mountain house where the partisan formation stayed, they heard the footsteps. Spillo went and looked out the hole in the door, recognized Pino's whistle, and opened it. The two of them came in, drenched to the bone and carrying the odor of stagnant humidity. They were immediately wrapped up in the warm breath of the fire, in the weak light of the gas lamp.

"Hello," said Brandonisio, the commander of the company.

"Quite a night," the new one murmured. He slipped off his swollen raincoat and extended his hands toward the fire.

"This guy," said Pino, "has been sent by the SAP of Castelluccio. He went into battle, so now they recognize him around there. Red said that you should use him here, because he can't stay over there anymore. Greetings to all!"

"Fine," said Brandonisio. "And now warm yourselves and rest. You, Savio, give them something to eat. We don't have much," he added as if excusing himself.

But in the meantime in the kitchen there was a lot of hustle and bustle. The partisans spoke to Pino, asking him for news of this one and that one, and Savio had already brought a plate of ricotta and a soup bowl full of dark broth to the table. He cut some slices of bread and immersed them in the boiling liquid. Pino and the new guy started to eat with gusto. They were bent over their bowls and they moved their spoons up and down rapidly. After the ricotta, Savio poured each one a little glass of wine, carefully, so as not to lose one drop.

"Oh, I feel great," Pino said, and he turned the chair to put his feet on the andirons. He pulled a small bag of tobacco and cigarette papers out of his pocket and offered to all around.

"I have a pack of cigarettes," said the new guy, and everybody stared at him. He rustled in the raincoat and pulled out a box of Serraglio and put it on the table. "Take them all," a small smile flickered over his lips. "I don't smoke."

Maybe because of that little smile, he didn't come off as nice. He had a face that was both well-fed and wanting, and it was all curves. The mouth with the corners turned down, the nostrils of the nose, the eyes, the eyebrows, and this gave him an air of astonishment, but cold and almost haughty, as if he were perpetually surprised by something of which he disapproved. And with that shadow of a useless smile, it was worse. He said his mother was from Ferrara and his father was Roman, and indeed he had a strange pronunciation, artificial, with strains of a Venetian cadence and a slow, southern drawl. But the partisans in the formation were accustomed to all languages, and they paid no attention. They had learned to understand each other even with the two Czechs—the "Dear Blonds" as they affectionately called them for their quiet and delicate goodness.

"His battle name is 'Quarto,'" said Pino.

They showed him his place in the big house on the bales of straw. They gave him a blanket and a sack, changed the guard in the kitchen, and then everyone went to bed.

The house was up high on a windswept hill. It was a magnificent place, as far as places go. The inhabitants had gone down into town, and they were working as *staffette*, good people, trustworthy, and safe comrades. From up there you could see a long way, beyond the steep slope where the sheltered mule path went uphill again into the woods. There was a nude terrain of gullies, rocks, and landslides. Down at the bottom, in that hard circle of steep and stingy earth, a village clung. The street divided it in two, and it was exposed in two long, white curves until it was lost in the gray crags at the bend.

"A fortress," said Brandonisio, who had been an artilleryman in the war in Greece. They kept the two machine guns trained on the exits. No one would get by there. They had arms and ammunition in abundance but little to eat. They adapted to everything like brothers, twelve Italians and two foreigners. Now with the new arrival, there were fifteen of them.

It wasn't as if he were disrespectful or undisciplined, that Quarto. Because with Brandonisio there was no fooling around. But his presence in the house was awkward from the very first day.

He talked too much for the taste of the partisans, who were already aged by the war and used to the silence. He hummed to himself unknown melodies and monotones that sometimes seemed to be church songs. Spillo, who was the happiest of the bunch, called him "the sacristan" under his breath, and that nickname stuck when they spoke of him in his absence. The rest had nothing to say; to them, he was even courageous. Two or three times he offered himself voluntarily to go into action on the road against the German trucks. He behaved well and didn't appear either demoralized or tired on his return. To the contrary, he seemed to be on the edge of a light euphoria. He went over the details of the undertaking, bringing up memories and other facts, and he had a hard time sleeping, such was his desire to discuss.

"Stop!" Ol' Tom said to him one evening. "It's not like we did the Voyage of the Thousand ourselves! Forget about it, would you, Quarto?"*

He almost said "sacristan" but caught himself in time. From that time forward, the partisan Quarto became withdrawn and silent, like almost all the others. He no longer even sang the usual songs. He worked hard; when he chopped wood you could see a great force in the muscles of his arms, maybe even disproportionate

* The reference is to Garibaldi's historic voyage to unite Italy. The "Thousand Men" traveled from Liguria to Sicily for the unification, ironically from a town named Quarto.

to his minute body. He lowered the axe as if taken by an angry urge.

It was one of the Dear Blonds, the tall one, Frantisek, who went secretly with Ol' Tom into the dark archway of the barn.

"That 'un," he said as he indicated Quarto in the courtyard, intent on cutting brambles for the fireplace, "speak German."

"What?" exclaimcd Ol' Tom, but Frantisek put a finger to his lips. Then he explained that he knew the German language well, having studied it in Vienna, and that the other Czech partisan understood it a bit, too. One morning he was translating some German phrases written on a little house and had heard Quarto speak "with many *deutsch* word."

"He no know I speak German. I not to say." He looked at Tom with his light blue eyes, a child's eyes in that burned and dry skin on his face, and concluded, "You decide."

It was his same old answer, "You decide!" He and the other Dear Blond trusted the Italian partisans implicitly.

"You decide, you decide!" Ol' Tom grumbled to himself for the rest of the day. He didn't know what to do. It didn't seem a very important thing, and not very nice, as if there were now doubts cast on Pino's word, since he'd brought that man up on Red's order. "The fact of the matter is that one understands damn little, with these foreign languages." Before night fell, he didn't feel like ruminating over his thoughts in bed, so he took Brandonisio aside and told him everything. With the result that now there were two who did not enjoy their sleep that night.

One day as spring was starting with an occasional leaf on the bushes, Quarto disappeared. They searched for him in the house, they called him with whistles in the undergrowth. The Dear Blonds were more agitated. "We go, find him," they said.

Brandonisio put an end to the commotion with two shouts. He stationed the men at the machine guns and gave other curt orders that everyone be ready to move.

"I never did like that one," Spillo said.

"Silence!" yelled Ol' Tom. "Everyone in his place, and quiet!"

In the house on the hill it looked like no one was left.

Brandonisio went down the mule path in leaps, followed by Corporal and by Fusel. He swore like a trooper. Coming out of the woods, he looked all around the valley, turning with the binoculars. He couldn't see anything; even the town seemed deserted.

"He's a damned spy," he said all of a sudden. "I was stupid. I didn't want to believe it. Now I'm sure."

A sharp whistle caught him from above. It was Spillo, who was running down from the crag, shouting, "Brandonisio, wait for me! Brandooo!"

He reached them all sweaty. "That bastard!" he shouted. "Shit! I found his documents. He's from Bolzano. The Blonds were right. He knows German."

"Get down," ordered Brandonisio, who had become suddenly cool and extremely calm. And in that exact moment a dark group of people appeared at the bend.

"That's Sandro from the house," Spillo said, who could see well from far away. And indeed, one man was running up ahead. They met each other panting.

"We took the man you had up there," the peasant said as soon as he got his voice back. "He was talking in the piazza with one of the Fascists. Then the Germans came, but he escaped. He was running toward here, he was taking the road. We cut across. My son grabbed him. Now you take him because we can't keep him."

He continued to explain as the partisans hurried down.

"Get lost, all of you. Leave town," shouted Brandonisio. "Now we'll take care of things."

Corporal, Fusel, and Spillo had the man of the quick smile between them, but he certainly was no longer smiling.

"Get the civilians out!" Brandonisio shouted again. In a second, it was only the partisans left with their prisoner. A profound silence descended on the mountain as the sound of the footsteps of those who were leaving faded away.

"You . . . and your damned dirty face," Spillo said quietly and he landed two violent smacks on those obnoxiously curved contours.

"Stop!" ordered Brandonisio. "That's not the way we're going to do it."

The other two had taken the man between them and they were tying his hands together with a strap.

"Don't touch him!" Brandonisio said again. "We're not like the Black Brigades."

A rumble rose from the valley; the street below was

gray with German vehicles. The first was a tank; it turned in place, the guns pointed toward the mountain. They had seen it from above and a blast of machine gun fire was heard.

"Go on up, hurry!" Brandonisio shouted. "We won't be able to maintain our position."

They hurried down, slipping along the rocks of the mule path and dragging Quarto behind, now pale as a corpse. In the courtyard in front of the house the whole company was assembled.

"Traitor!" said Fusel as they came up from the steep bank.

"Put your machine guns away," Brandonisio shouted. "Leave everything and retreat with your weapons."

"And this?" Spillo yelled, pushing the bound man ahead of him. A gunshot rustled the air and was lost in the foliage of the woods.

"Break out," Brandonisio commanded calmly. "You, stop a moment!" he ordered those with the machine guns.

They understood. The Dear Blonds, Ol' Tom, and Savio turned around and lined up as if for an exercise.

"Fire!" a clear, loud voice said. The man tumbled, crashing onto the white dust of the courtyard.

"March! Go on!" the commander bellowed.

The tanks shot from the street, aiming higher. One shot shattered at the top of the hill, hitting the house straight on.

The Big Opportunity

The boy saw before him the trim figure of a woman who walked with an agile step. "Excuse me, miss, may I?" he said as he caught up to her, and she hurried along without turning her head.

"Excuse me, miss," he insisted. "I wanted to tell you something." He had reached her side and he looked at her. She wasn't as young as she looked; indeed, she had a small face that was delicately faded.

"Why don't you leave me in peace?" she said, stopping suddenly. Even her voice seemed old and worn out, veiled by hoarseness. Only her eyes were still beautiful.

"Excuse me," the boy said. "I wanted to ask you a question."

It was a haggard evening in November. In the middle of the ruins of the bombings, via Riva di Reno wound along the gray canal; the water ran through the shining stones of the washerwomen, now vanished. Few people had remained to live on that street since it had been hit, leaving massive debris from the Main Hospital.

"Go on," she murmured, as if resigned.

"I'm looking for a place to sleep," the boy said. "Even a mattress in a corridor, or a cot. I come from the countryside. I can't go home." He smiled timidly and his face had a surprised, infantile look.

"Really," he added. "I don't know what to do; I don't know anyone. But I've got the money to pay."

They slowly walked along the length of the broken wall. They were about to step into a puddle when he, with a light pressure on her arm, pushed her aside. "Better not to get wet," he said. "My shoes are broken."

"Me too," the woman confessed, and from that moment on it seemed as if they'd known each other a long time. They talked of the war and the sacrifices, of the danger and all the things they lacked. In the city, people were starving, yet the Allied offensive had been postponed until spring.

They came to a large front door and stopped. She looked around the colorless landscape, the mute water of the canal, the ruins of the Main Hospital that in the fog looked like a destroyed fortress. She said hesitantly, "If you want to come up to my apartment . . ."

She opened the door with a large key and pushed open the double door. "Wait, I'll find the matches. The light in the hall isn't working."

It was the boy who struck the matches against the wall as they went up the stairs. And indeed, it seemed to him only right to have more faith in her, a woman who had welcomed him, a stranger, in this way, into a silent house in a section of town that was practically uninhabited.

"My name is Vincenzo Ravadesi," he said. "I was with my aunt's family. My parents died when I was little . . ."

"You'll tell me later," the woman whispered on the

landing, busy with the locks. "Make yourself comfortable."

From a small kitchen, they passed into a room with a sharp, white light. Everything in the apartment was there in that one room, space enough for a woman alone.

"Look," she said with a kind of excitement in her voice. "I'm not a prostitute. Don't get any ideas just because I let you come up here so easily. I work and earn my freedom."

"But of course," Vincenzo said. "I didn't think otherwise, believe me . . ."

He was in fact sincerely happy. A prostitute, that poor little, pale woman! It was too sad and cruel to think.

"How should I address you? Miss . . . ?" he asked politely.

"Marta," she replied, taking off her gray little coat, too light for the season. "Marta Giani. I'm a nurse at the hospital."

She went back and forth across the room, preparing coffee on a gas burner. "A poor substitute," she explained, pouring from the boiling coffee pot. "Grain and roasted barley. Little body, but at least it won't make you sick."

She smiled and spoke slowly, rather artificially and sophisticated, as if she wanted somehow to make up for not being beautiful and no longer young. She poured the hot, black liquid and sipped hers in little gulps, lightly raising her cup, her hand unfurled with her pinky in the air.

"Now tell me," she said. "Tell me about yourself."

But it seemed Vincent had little to say about himself, or at least he didn't intend to tell very much. He told her he'd been orphaned while still a child and that he'd been raised in a boarding school. He had a diploma as a surveyor, and he lived with an aunt in a small town in the provinces.

"I ran away this morning," he exclaimed after a pause, with a changed, trembling voice. "I can't stay there anymore. My aunt is a Fascist; my cousin is a Fascist in the Black Brigades. They say I'm a draft dodger, that up 'til now they've kept me hidden and now they're sorry. They want me to go present myself to the authorities . . ." He looked the woman in the face; she was white as a ghost. "And me, go present myself to those assassins, to those delinquents, goddamn it, I won't go."

Now he was speaking loudly and clearly, with a crack in his voice that was almost a cry.

"Shhhh, speak softly," she said, almost breathless.

They stopped to listen, but there was a closed silence around them, compact, like in the desert.

"I'm sorry," Marta whispered. "I'm afraid of the neighbors."

"No, I'm sorry," said Vincenzo. "I shouldn't have. I'm in your home."

He felt both happy and displaced, immersed in an acute sense of unreality. He saw that small, unknown woman next to him, and he felt he owed her something because she had welcomed him without fear. He suddenly realized he wanted her, just as she was, not beautiful and not young. He caressed her head and pulled her to him tightly. She let him do it, devoid of any defense but also of any eagerness. She only reached out her hand to turn off the light. And love was a poor thing in that cold and dark room.

They found themselves happy afterwards, talking together. Marta made coffee again; they smoked some cigarettes made with dark tobacco in big papers that wouldn't stay closed. They laughed and even slept a little next to each other on the couch that served as a bed. A mild, white dawn began to brighten the openings in the shutters. Vincenzo shrugged off the sleep and fatigue and washed himself for a long time in the kitchen with the freezing water from the faucet.

Another day had begun, an uncertain, foggy, confusing day. He didn't know where to go or what to do. "Here I'm safe," he thought, combing his thick, almost blond hair. "But I can't stay here." He felt uncomfortable, almost ashamed, and it seemed he would never find the right words to say good-bye to Marta. He felt for an instant the temptation to leave very quietly without waking her, but he told himself that would be a cowardly act. In that moment, a rumble began, dull and heavy, and it enveloped the air of the house, the street, and it vanished high up in jolts, like thunder.

Marta jumped in her sleep and ran toward the window. She couldn't see anything; the room looked out on an expanse of rubble cut by the slow running of the canal. The roar repeated, this time louder and longer, like many repeated hits, fused together.

"Cannons," Vincenzo said. "Who's shooting?"

"I don't know. I'm afraid," whispered Marta, and she closed the window.

Vincenzo was also afraid, but he didn't want to stay there motionless, useless, and ignorant of where the danger was coming from. "I'm getting out of here," he said. "Excuse me, and good-bye."

"I don't want to stay here alone," Marta implored. "Let me come with you!"

She threw her coat on quickly and they went down the stairs. Behind the closed doors they heard buzzing and words. Certainly all the tenants were awake and agitated.

On the street very few people passed, and it was cold. On the surface, it appeared that people were coming and going calmly. Another hammering noise burst somewhere nearby on the opposite side of the street. Machine-gun fire. It stopped for a moment, and then started up again, insistent blasts like a hailstorm. Some people stopped, and others got together in groups with words and gestures that were increasingly perplexed and excited.

"They're shooting on the Lame Gate," one person said.

"But even down there noise could be heard," another added, "and a little while ago there was cannon fire."

All of a sudden it seemed like they were on a silent island, surrounded by a great, threatening wall of shots. Vincenzo and Marta reached the group as it was splitting up. "What is it? What's going on?" But by now everyone was filled with a doubtful anxiety, where fear began to take root. A tall man with no coat but a faded jacket and a dark scarf around his neck passed near Vincenzo. He looked at him, and he seemed vaguely familiar; then Vincenzo began to follow him, with Marta on his arm. Now he was really bothered by her, by her step, by her light, anxious breathing. He was trying to think of a way to free himself of her, and at the same time he didn't want to lose sight of the tall man, who was practically running. And then the man turned as he was going around a corner and slowed his step immediately.

"You're Ravadesi, right?" he said, and he continued without waiting for an answer. "I've just come from San Giorgio. I know you ran away so you wouldn't have to go with the Fascists. Your aunt is a hyena, she really is, like that rogue of a cousin of yours. They're looking for you, and in town that's all they're talking about. Be careful not to get caught!"

The deep thunder of the cannon passed through the gray air. The response of machine-gun fire began again from the opposite side of the street.

"They're attacking today," said the tall man. "The Germans are attacking in force. But they'll find it difficult, with the partisans."

He stood there a moment, indecisive, staring at Vincenzo. "I don't have time now. Go and hide." He turned toward Marta, observed her, and seemed satisfied. "Hide him, ma'am. If they find him, they'll kill him."

He took up his brisk pace again in the silence, and was soon submerged by a new wave of shots.

"Wait for me! Wait for me! I'm coming with you," Vicenzo shouted suddenly. He freed himself from Marta's arm and ran down the narrow street, turning into the road where the tall man had disappeared.

"Vincenzo, Vincenzo!" Marta called with her fragile voice. She wanted to run, but one of her heels got caught in the hollow of a broken stone; she lost her balance and pitched forward, but she didn't fall. Her ankle hurt from the effort. She leaned against the wall, trembling, and pain ran through her legs to her kidneys; this mixed with another pain, also physical, which was beating in her chest—Vincenzo's escape, without a word to her. Indeed, by pushing her away, maybe he was the one who had given her the push that had almost made her break her foot.

She began again, little by little, with her usual habit of disappointments. She considered the fact that she was alone in the cold in the midst of the crossfire. The blasts from unknown origins could easily reach her; one stray bullet would be enough to kill her, just like that, against that wall, unknown and unremembered by anyone. She started to cry, feeling sorry for herself. It seemed she had never amounted to anything in life, and that this time she had lost her big opportunity.

She awakened in the middle of the night because someone was knocking on her door. "It's Vincenzo," she thought, as she slipped on her bathrobe. She opened the door with that thought, without asking who it was, and she found before herself a small, fat man.

"Are you Miss Marta?" he asked. "Vincenzo sent me. I

have my comrade here." He seemed to pull him out of the shadow of the landing, a thin, brown boy with eyes that were almost closed, and he was very pale.

"Come in," said Marta.

"He's hurt and we have to hide him," the fat man explained. In that very moment the boy slipped to the floor along the edge of the door; he would have fallen if the other hadn't held him up. Together with Marta, they brought him inside and put him on the couch.

"He's bad," she said agitatedly.

"Vincenzo told me that you're a nurse, right?" said the fat man. "Take a look at him."

But the boy revived a bit. "No, it's nothing," he whispered. "I've lost a lot of blood but the bullet came out. They've already given me medicine. I need a bit of rest, out of that burning hell."

"Please, be careful," the fat man said. He shook Marta's hand and left.

The rest of the night Marta spent on the armchair, wrapped in a blanket, watching the sleeping boy. Outside she could hear roars and shots, but she was no longer afraid. "Enough already," she said. "Enough. Something will happen. We will all make it through this nightmare. Either we'll save ourselves, or we'll all die. But let it be for something worthwhile, something useful. They will have to explain to me, these people, why they risk their lives. I'll give my own life, too, it's worth so little." The same old tears stung her eyes, but she felt better, clearer, more lucid. Her rhetorical imagination gave way to the brutal realities of the war. She reproached herself for not having understood sooner, for not having taken part from the beginning in this undertaking that now seemed to her so necessary and fascinating. She remembered now having said no to certain proposals of collaboration that some of her colleagues at the hospital had advanced. For example, to offer her house. No, she had said, I don't want to lose my freedom. But what freedom? To grow old in silence and alone?

Now she watched the sleeping, wounded boy. Maybe others would come and take refuge there. Vincenzo had found his way, he had gone with the partisans. Well she, too, would work to help them, she would be with them to the end, even to her death. With her old romantic spirit, she wanted to perform some act that would be more like her. She took down from the wall one of her photographs and wrote across it: "Vincenzo —7 novembre 1944."

From that day on she was never the same. She said it after the liberation, happy and aware, "I can say that I was born at the battle of the Lame Gate." She laughed and straightened her hair that had begun to thin and turn gray.

The House on the Ice

The house was in a barren valley, sunk between two rough, rocky ridges. The solid color of the earth hid it better than if it had been covered with trees and plants. As low and lopsided as it was, with a roof of gray slate and the windows barred, it blended in at the ground level with the folds of the gullies. The street that led to the house was also invisible, not much more than a path in a desert of stones. The partisans had discovered it one night in the rain, during a reconnaissance mission. It was a good shelter to hide in. They brought two wounded men and one sick man, four guards, and a student in his fifth year of medical school whom everyone called Doctor.

In the house lived Quinto, the peasant, and his wife, Rosalia, a few sheep, and a mule. Down lower, where the earth widened toward the sun, they had a small field of wheat, a vegetable garden near the river, and a slope planted with corn. From there, from the courtyard where the scrawny hens lived, their only son had left. Alfeo was twenty years old and tall, big, robust. He was a peaceful boy; he had a girlfriend in town. But he went off to die, a soldier, in the big Russian winter—him of all people, who had an instinctive fondness for the Russians. He never would have wanted to attack them.

Rosalia was small and dark, protected in her silent mourning. She welcomed the partisans gladly; she opened her rooms to them, prepared all the beds. Her husband, Quinto, as if erased from the active world by the death of their son, did everything she wanted. He was tall, thin, inattentive. He worked better when he was told what to do, lacking his own initiative, and he always mumbled to himself. Then the December cold came and the house was besieged by snow. Every day it seemed to sink lower into a blue layer of ice, into a transparent, rarefied prison. But it was still solid, like the crude light that enveloped the mountain.

"Damn, it's cold," said Gigio, the oldest one, who by the consent of the group had assumed the command. He had come in from his turn as guard, which they had not given up for safety's sake. Right away Danilo replaced him, slamming the door behind him. He walked up and down in the glimmer of an implacable moon that hung in the sky like a huge medallion. He was surrounded by a polar landscape, with a snow that was both scintillating and opaque, depending on the frozen waves of the terrain. "I could die here," he thought. "We'll never get out of here." He forced himself to imagine vivid colors—reds, blues, greens, warm colors, fields in the sunlight, grass dried by the heat, buzzing with bees. The frost burned his fingers like fire, his skin ached with shivers that wracked his body, while his feet were like two inert stones to be dragged along. "One hundred degrees in the shade," he murmured through chattering teeth. "How nice, one hundred, one hundred and twenty degrees in the shade, the sun in your bones, the sweat in your eyes! . . . What the hell am I doing here? Who the hell is going to come up tonight on this damned mountain? I'm going home." He would have liked to, but he was ashamed because of his comrades, because of Gigio especially, because Gigio had been out here like him, without complaining. He had said, "Damn, it's cold," and that's all, with his beautiful amused smile.

"Not everybody's the same," he said loudly, and his voice resounded in the hard, resplendent air, and in that very moment he heard a sound, a noise, like the pounding of feet on the path. He saw two black figures coming toward him, bent over, and a blast of fear ran to his face under the wool of the cap.

"Who goes there? Halt, or I'll shoot!"

He no longer felt the cold while he feverishly slipped the machine gun off his shoulder and pushed the magazine cartridge in.

"The wind is blowing here . . ." sang a well-known voice.

"Is that you, Fino?" asked Danilo, all of his limbs relaxing in relief.

"It's me," Fino replied. "I've come to the pole. You're on ice, up here."

Near one another, the small clouds of their breath mingled. Fino's smelled lightly of grappa.

"Commander's orders," he said, stomping his feet on the frozen snow. "I've brought my cousin, a distant cousin, up. His name's Gino, eighteen years old, draft dodger. Beat it, snail, or you'll die up here."

In the few steps they took to get to the house, the boy leaned on Danilo's arm. He felt the violent shaking through the material, a rough groan as the door opened.

Inside, the wood burned in the fireplace. The house cat was sleeping on the hearth with his back to the flames, and his gray fur shone as if it were about to catch fire. On the cot in the corner, a partisan was stretched out. He lifted himself up on one elbow and said, "Who is it?"

"It's me," Danilo replied. "We have visitors. Get up, Fafita."

The boy, completely wrapped up, let himself down onto a chair. He stroked his legs with his hands and clapped his palms together, saying softly, "It hurts . . . It hurts . . . !" In the weak light of the gas lamp, his face was white. He started sweating, complaining, and his forehead was colorless and bathed in sweat.

"Do something," said Fino. "Give him something to drink. He's been in a cellar for days and days. He couldn't take the cold."

Danilo opened the door toward the inside and called loudly, "Doctor!"

Fafita paced up and down in the kitchen, as heavy as a boulder, and said, "So outside there's no one on guard, and you're in here jabbering. And just like you came up here, so, too, can the *deutsch* to attack us. Because they're never cold, those Germans." He wrapped himself in his country cape with a decisive, wide gesture. "Give me your gun, Danilo."

He grabbed it out of his hands and went out swearing; in the same moment the Doctor entered from the stairs. The boy near the fire slumped straight down to the floor in a faint.

More ice, more snow. A fishbowl life, looking out the windows into a liquid light. The two men, wounded in the legs, were healing too slowly; the sick man stayed in the heat of his own body, well-preserved in bed. Apart from that, he'd started coughing and had fever again. The Doctor was short on medicine and invented hopes.

"There's never been such a bad winter," Quinto the peasant said, vague and disorderly, and yet trying to be helpful, looking for wood.

"There was a worse winter," murmured Rosalia, thinking about her poor little boy, dead in Russia.

The men crowded together in the only small, warm place each one had around the insufficient fire. Their nerves were strained; they preferred risk to inactivity. After three or four days they had to start rationing the provisions, and there was always something to say about it, depending on the character of one or the other person.

One morning, when the sun was shining brilliantly like a white, blinding flame on the undulating crests of ice, the Doctor opened the window suddenly, and for a second he was dazzled; he felt his eyes burn; he hadn't slept and his head hurt. "We can no longer stay up here," he decided. "Or I'll end up sick, too." He was conscious of his heavy responsibility. "Where to go?" he wondered with a shiver running up his spine. He had no answer and ran down to the kitchen where he gathered his companions together. Among their dark faces, the one of the boy stood out, for he was still whitened from his long stay in the hiding spot.

"Listen to what I'm telling you," the Doctor exclaimed suddenly. "We've got to get out of here. I know it's dangerous, but it's worse to stay. In a little while we'll be out of medicine and out of food. Let's make stretchers to transport Cencio and the others. And let's send a *staffetta* to the command post to ask where we should go. I don't want to see them die, my three patients. Get it?"

He added in a quiet voice, "Not one of us is going to die. No one here is going to die."

There was a deep pause, then other voices exploded all together in the excitement of deciding what to do, in not staying any longer waiting for the dawn after the evening, and the evening after the dawn, across interminable empty spaces.

"Quiet!" shouted Gigio. "One at a time!"

Even Rosalia came forward, small and black, wringing her big, embarrassed hands. She looked the partisans in the face one by one and watched their mouths intently, like a deaf-mute.

It happened suddenly, and no one knows exactly why. Maybe some age-old family feud. Fino and the boy were fighting; most likely, Fino had attacked him with bitter words. Then, all of a sudden, the boy let loose: he hauled off and gave Fino a punch in the nose that knocked him staggering against the wall.

"Good God," Gigio screamed. "Are you crazy?" But he couldn't manage to keep the boy back as he ran to the door, opened it wide, and then disappeared, closing it behind him with a thud.

Right away Gigio, Danilo, and the Doctor went out into the night. But they could see nothing: the night sky was dark and closed, the ice without light. They might as well have been blindfolded. "Gino! Gino!!" they called. And they waited. It seemed they could hear the faraway sound of running, but everything died in the echo of their voices. It was so cold that the mountain resounded like a crystal. They came back en masse, dumbstruck, but the Doctor said right away, "We have to find him. If he's out in this blasted subzero weather he'll die . . . If he manages to get down the mountain, the Germans or the Fascists will get him."

When he saw Fino's face before him, a fiery rage took him over. "You and your stupid family nonsense! Now go and look for him! We'll all go. You better hope he doesn't die, hope with your whole filthy heart that's good only for screwing life, because if that boy dies, remember, if he dies, I'll have you shot. Now, get out of here!"

They threw their jackets and coats on, and they all went out. Only Quinto stayed behind, answering the three sick men's requests; they were asking loudly about what was going on.

"Am I out of my mind?" the Doctor said, coming back in. "I lost control. I was about to abandon these boys here."

He shouted toward the stairway. "It's nothing, nothing. Sleep!" and then to Quinto, "Where's Rosalia?"

"With them," the peasant answered, distractedly. "She went to look for the boy."

And that's how the wait began, with the gas lamp that was smoking. Every so often Quinto raised the wick and the light came up clearly. The Doctor was pacing up and down like a prisoner, talking to himself. With the others gone and his sick men sleeping, he had never felt so alone. Finally he heard some motion outside and he opened the door. Slow shadows were coming forward, carrying something. In front of them came Rosalia, running, all white with snow.

"It's him, it's him, he's alive," she said hurriedly. And she went straightaway to throw kindling on the fire. Gigio and Fino were carrying the inanimate boy.

"Here," said the Doctor, "on the table. Undress him."

He was slender, white on the dark wood, only his face appeared red, swollen from having been out all day chopping wood in the reflection of the sun on the snow. He was barely breathing, and his eyelashes fluttered slowly as if for light chills. His skin was immobile and cold.

"Come on!" said the Doctor. He had become calm once more, and he moved around the outstretched body in an efficient manner, helped by Gigio.

"Will he live?" Fino asked under his breath, and very pale under his tan.

"Go out and whistle for the others to return, make yourself useful," the Doctor told him, sharply. And he quickly disappeared.

Rosalia was at the head of the table, near the immobile head of the boy. She was trying slowly to put a small spoon between his clenched teeth. The tangy smell of grappa hung in the air. Finally she managed to do it, and his jaw relaxed, the liquid went down and spilled out a bit. It slipped down his throat, and the boy coughed weakly.

"He opened his eyes," Rosalia whispered. Even the Doctor had seen, and he felt himself break out in a cold sweat, a sweat of joy.

"And now Fino has been saved, too," he said.

Wool Socks

Silveria set out along the carriage road, pedaling on her old bicycle. She was a young woman, beautiful, with that kind of delicate beauty of the Comacchio valley that resembles the slim loveliness of the figures on Etruscan amphorae from Spina, the submerged city. An unexpected force motivated her dark-skinned body, like all those of her race. She wore black, with a large kerchief pulled forward on her head and tucked under in back, tightly framing her smooth, brown face. In the plains of Ferrara many women, even the young ones, wore black; Silveria with even more reason because she was a widow. Her husband had been assassinated by the Fascists one evening in May while he was returning home. They shot him down against a wall with a burst of machine-gun fire. He had been a Communist leader, organizing companies of partisans in the valley. After his death they named the brigade for him.

From that day on, after having cried until there were no more tears, Silveria entered a partisan formation. A grim and violent winter had taken the place of autumn; the snow got stuck in the slimy, wet mud of the marshes; and the immense water iced over, silver and brilliant under a faraway sky, which was both gloomy and bright.

A geometric landscape, devastated, deserted, like you see in dreams.

Silveria continued on with difficulty against the wind, pushing her worn-out wooden clogs against the pedals. The patched tires rustled against the uneven surface and she bounced badly on the seat. It seemed she might turn over on the bank of hard yellow grass dotted with dirty snow.

"Oh, oh!" a voice shouted in the silence, and Silveria responded with the same shout, "Oh, oh!" so soft and high-pitched that it could have been taken for a valley bird's song. Barely discernible in the thick fog was a house; it seemed to hang in the air, suspended like a boat sailing adrift. Silveria bent over the handlebars; her hands, red with cold, hurt. With a sudden push, she quickened her pedaling and came through an opening in the hedge onto the stones of the courtyard.

Inside the big, black kitchen a fire of twigs and underbrush burned in the hearth.

"Thank goodness, you came early," said a woman, who was stirring something in a small pan on the fire.

"It's freezing out there, Mamma," Silveria answered, and she extended her arms toward the warmth. She rubbed the fingers of her hands hard, such was the pain.

"They feel like needles," she said in the dialect. Then she took off her coat, undid the kerchief. The lustrous waves of her hair appeared, her forehead, her ears. She suddenly seemed slimmer and younger.

"They're all upstairs," her mother indicated with a gesture toward the ceiling.

"I'm going," Silveria answered.

Opening the door toward the stairs, she added: "We'll have to do it quickly. Go and come back before curfew."

In the room upstairs was her bed and a few pieces of furniture. Six women were sitting around a table with an oil lamp in the middle. They were knitting in the weak light, but they were so skilled and fast that they didn't look at their work. Another two, almost in complete darkness, were unwinding the wool from the spindle, stamping with the tips of their toes the regular movement of the small plank that made the wheel turn: a quiet, continual humming, like the sound of a light rainfall.

"So?"

"Did you get it, Silveria?"

"How did it go?" They murmured, as if they were afraid to be heard, even if the house was closed up and isolated in the middle of the countryside.

"I got it," Silveria answered. "The shepherd is giving us the wool. He's already shorn, and he's waiting for us."

"Is there a lot?" asked a girl, lifting her pretty, chubby face from her work.

"Three bags," Silveria replied. "Thirty kilos per bag. It's not long, but it's pretty. It's cheap; we'll have to wash it."

"My steeping pit is full," another said. "I'll bring the water into the house, and we'll be done soon. To dry it we can hang it in the barn."

"We'll have to keep a few kilos here," said Silveria. "Otherwise tomorrow there won't be enough to work."

"Sure," said one of the women from the spindle, indicating a small white mound at her feet. "This is the last."

"Let's go then," said Silveria. "The time is right."

They all got up, putting the wool socks on the table. They were big and thick; some were only halfway done, others almost finished. The knitting needles stuck in the rows of stitches gleamed in the lamp light.

"To get to the shepherd's, only four of us need to go," said one, who appeared to be the oldest. "The rest of you, it's better if you go home now, each one on her own. And let's put the stuff away."

The socks disappeared into a chest, together with the balls of wool. The women descended the stairs, tying their shawls and kerchiefs on.

"Good evening."

"Bye, Vincenza!"

"See you tomorrow!"

They spoke in whispers as they went to get their bicycles behind the wall of the barn; they slipped away, turning onto the country road. The cold took them into its icy shroud; the fog hid them.

A little while later Silveria and her three companions left, following the embankment toward the valley. They pedaled slowly, dark shadows in the dark evening. Mamma Vincenza followed them with her gaze from the door, until they blended into the empty light of the sky.

The following day a pale sun slipped between the trees, lighting on the wet stones, weakly sparkling against the glass of the windows.

In Silveria's room the spindles were working hard, chock full of wool, the knitting needles tinkled in the girls' hands. Every so often one intertwined the stitches, broke the yarn. The finished sock was there, on the table, waiting for its mate; that didn't take long. They all made them the same, all big. They paired them, stretching them out and beating them to make them softer; they folded them on the bottom of the chest and put the heavy wedding linens on top. The house was always quiet and closed, except for the windows and the kitchen door. Upstairs, where the girls were working, they kept the shutters ajar. Looking from the outside, it seemed like no one was home.

They ate in the kitchen, all together around the big table. A house of only women. Silveria had returned, come back to her mother's, after her husband had been killed. He had organized the work for the partisans hiding in the valley, the deserters buried in the reclaimed land in certain holes of dry culverts where they could breathe through a stove pipe, or scattered in reed huts on their bare backs in the middle of the water of great stagnant mirrors. An unnatural life, where boats, trucks, ferries, and barges were the only good means for the supply of food and arms. The cold was the worst enemy, and an impious one. After Alexander's proclamation, in which he'd said with unconscious simplicity, "Break up the partisan bands and go home until springtime," the Anglo-Americans were basking by the seaside, wintering in Ravenna, and the Germans who were occupying the towns were having a good time in their lodgings.

Silveria's old girlhood home had been chosen because it was solitary and distant, and the women came on bicycle, crossing the fields. They got together to knit, socks mostly, and socks of good warm lamb's wool, because feet were always cold, both the feet of those who went into combat to blow up German trucks in the important streets, and the feet of the others, who remained underground, white and trembling like the grain grown in the dark for the day of the sepulchers at Easter in the churches.

Back and forth, in the sonorous and transparent frost, or when the chill was soft with penetrating, wet fog, the women went looking for wool at the shepherds'. They prevailed due to the sheer force of their insistence, or with cash; the frequent refusals originating from greed or from fear. These were mountain people, diffident and unknown, who during the winter took the flocks to graze on the plains. Little by little they were persuaded by a new necessity, by a change in ideas that had upset their absent and primordial lives, marked by a regime that was centuries old. One way or another, they ended up giving them the wool. And the women worked it, from the oily shearing to the yielding manufacture of the socks, and then they reached the dangerous operation of the delivery. They worked in the dark, shrewd and taciturn, because they were afraid above all else of spies. Spying had resulted in the ambush on Silveria's husband and countless other irreparable problems.

"Where are you bringing this?" Vincenza asked, when she had crammed quite a pile of socks into a bag.

"This one's going far," Silveria answered. "To the Big House of Rome."

A little brunette, her hair all tight curls, jumped from her chair. "I'll go, Silveria, I beg of you . . . I beg of you . . ."

She raised her voice above the disapproving buzz of the others, so much so that Vincenza let out a rude "Ssss . . !"

"You know that Gino, my fiancé, is at Rome's place," the girl insisted. "Send me, Silveria . . ."

"You're too tiny," said another in dialect.

"Too small," Vincenza confirmed.

She started to cry, bowing her head on her hands, until Silveria said, "But she's been a *staffetta* all summer for Mario. Didn't you know? In fact, her combat name is Tiny."

The reference to her dead husband made the decision right. Tiny stopped crying and took the bag, tightening the kerchief around her face that was a little pale but cheerful, without so much as a trace of the recent tears. She ran outside into the premature waning of light. It was barely five and already seemed like evening. It was drizzling light rain in the fog. The bicycle rustled on the icy ground.

"We shouldn't have let her go," Vincenza said under her breath, brushing a match along the fireplace to light the oil lamp.

Tiny went along with her warm bundle on her shoulder, driving with only one hand. She knew the road like her own house, rock by rock, bush by bush. She didn't meet anyone until the corner of the abandoned mill. She turned hard to take the path along the embankment and found herself face to face with two tall black figures.

"Get off," said one, and he turned the bike over; the other grabbed the bag from her arm. They seized her along with the bag and dragged her into the rubble. In the light of a flashlight she recognized two faces of Germans.

"Wool socks," said a third one, appearing in the light, and it was one of the Fascists of the town.

"Supplies," he added, turning to the Germans. "Partisan."

He made a vague gesture toward the valley, then let go with a slap across the face to the girl. "Where are you bringing these socks?" he asked. "Who's making them? Where do you meet, you filthy . . ."

The Germans laughed softly, bumping each other's elbows.

"Black market," Tiny stuttered, rubbing the cheek that had been struck.

"Ah ah, black market . . ." the Fascist said, and the Germans laughed harder.

"*Bella, bella, dolce amore* . . ." one said, his big hand falling on the girl's neck, rummaging through her curls.

"Wait," said the Fascist, "we have to make her tell . . ." he tried to help himself with gestures to make himself understood, but the German rose up, almost with rage.

"*Genug, basta, kamarad,* let me . . ." while the other split his sides laughing.

Wool Socks

Cries and screams filled the night, but they did not span the air. Cries, but not names, not of people, not of places. At Silveria's house they worked and waited; at the Big House of Rome they only waited. An unspoken anguish stretched from one place to the other, anguish for Tiny who had not arrived and had not returned. In the middle of the rubble she screamed and did not say anything. In the end, the three were so tired they even forgot to kill her.

At dawn, among white rags of fog, she staggered, bloodied, toward home. Wool socks pierced her black and blue forehead and were threaded through her hands and through her arms. In front of her, her lacerated clothes and small, slashed breasts.

The Last Action

Hundred came bounding down the mule path and the stones rolled and slipped under his shoes. He was making a hell of a noise. "Let's hope there's no Nazis around here," he thought, and in the meantime he touched the pistol he'd slipped under the left side of his jacket.*

Certainly it was a nice mission, the one he had that day, and it was the commander who had ordered him to do it. Go down to the town, be careful not to get caught by the Germans—don't worry about the Fascists, they'd all escaped already—and find two comrades who were working in a given spot, give them a short message, and come back to the brigade as fast as he could. Like that, a fast, coordinated action, and it could free the area, flush out the last of the stubborn, dangerous Germans who were hiding and sniping on the roads, bridges, and passageways, where the partisans continued to lose some of their best men.

Once they'd cleared out the Nazis, they'd leave to

* The custom of touching something made of metal *(Tocca ferro)* is to ward off bad luck, much like the Anglo-Saxon custom of "touching" or "knocking on" wood.

join the Allies on the front, which was only three kilometers away. They continued carpet bombing the territory with their planes and were tossing artillery like they were doing an exercise. He would tell them that if they wanted to advance, the village no longer had even a shadow of a German and had already been in the hands of the partisans for a few hours. Then the tanks, vehicles, cars, cranes, mobile repair units, cannon, heavy artillery, and mounted machine guns would have come by the tens, by the hundreds, by the thousands, and the line would have moved ahead that little bit that the partisans had conquered. And everything would begin again, up there.

Hundred was worried, though. It was his first individual mission, and it was very dangerous. Up to now he'd taken part in collective operations, courageous but without needing to use his brain, his readiness, and good sense, because he'd always been led by someone who knew more about it than him. This time he'd have to act alone and without even very much explanation from the commander. At a certain point, after several anxious questions, the answer he got was, "Take care of it yourself!" They knew in the brigade that the commander was a man of few words.

Going down the mule path, between the hedges of honeysuckle and blackberries that he knew like the rooms of his own house—how many girls he had taken up years past on Sunday evenings to kiss them without running into trouble!—it was becoming dark and cool. A still and timid autumn on the stingy hills of the

Apennines, the same old, hard grumbling of the front, to which everyone had become accustomed. It seemed impossible that it was about to end, that the Anglo-Americans were so close that they could be dragged on ahead, to push them further, liberating the plateaus that had been like a desert for so long, resigned and treacherous.

Hundred came out at Prati Segati and stopped a while to rest. He availed himself of the little fountain, taking a drink from a thin line of icy water that spouted from the rocks and was lost in the grass, leaving it clear and green in the midst of the darkness of the other grass that was almost dead from the grazing. Standing there drinking, he heard a noise behind a hazelnut tree, a rustling, not of some bird, but of some large animal. He checked his pistol and then passed the bush. He saw a woman stretched out as if she were sleeping, with her face resting on her folded arms.

"Hey, young woman, it gets cold in the evening!" he said, and he was suddenly afraid that maybe she was dead, and he shook her by a shoulder. But she wasn't dead and she turned toward him right away, and he recognized her as one from the town.

"Where are you going, Herman?" she asked, without surprise, turning lazily and putting a blade of grass in her mouth.

Hundred's real name was not at all to his liking, and hearing it spoken, even from one from his own village, bothered him. He was no longer used to it, and it seemed to him that his whole life he would now be called *Hundred,* like up there among the partisans.

"And you, what are you looking for out here? Are you alone? If a Nazi comes along, he'll have a good time."†

She chewed the blade of grass and stared at him. She was neither beautiful nor ugly. Her face was without color, her complexion uniform; eyebrows, eyelashes, and skin, round, pale eyes, a big mouth, well-formed, even if it concealed the flaw of some damaged teeth. She was staring at Hundred with those unwavering eyes, and the fact of the matter was that, for a long time now, there'd been no women in the brigade, and at twenty-two that is something to be missed.

"The Germans love me, but I love the partisans," the girl said, spitting out the blade of grass. And she turned over on her stomach again, but she turned her face, now more flushed, toward Hundred. And so he kissed her on her wide mouth, and then he grabbed her without difficulty, because she didn't defend herself, and he executed his act quickly, precisely, almost without pleasure. An action like any other in life.

"Shame on you!" the girl said.

"Shame on *you!*" Hundred answered jokingly, getting up, and already sorry for wasting time. Now she, too, got up and put on her red sweater that she'd laid on in the grass, adjusting her skirt.

"Wait a minute, no?" she whispered, looking for Hundred to hug him. But he had suddenly realized that it had gotten dark and the spring was pouring out

† The expression Viganò used, *farti la festa* ("*Se arriva un nazi ti fa la festa*"), means both "to have a good time (with you)" and "to kill (you)."

stronger; the hazelnut trees were black. There was only a little bit of light sky above the hills.

"Good God," he said. "Damn women! . . . Who told me to stop? . . . I should already be at Mentino and Tanon's!" He thrust the girl away from his chest. "You come along since you know the road. I have to run."

He hurtled down the mule path with the skill of one who has passed by there a million times since childhood when he went there with the cows and the sheep.

In town he found a great confusion. "The Americans are coming!" a man shouted at him with his eyes bulging from his head. The front had exploded and screamed, and the grenades were whistling over the houses as people were escaping to the countryside. Then a silent and invisible plane came, and they only realized it because it dropped a torch, and then another and another—a slow, white, open light, and in the town it was like daytime. And finally the rumble of the fighter-bombers was heard. They were coming fast, and they began a maelstrom of machine-gun fire; then they would climb and release the bombs. In the glow of the Bengal lights that were falling, they could see the houses that had been hit; and when it was all dark again, a fire started. Screams and shouts filled the night, the desperate rush of those who were looking for someone who had died in a bomb's sudden explosion or who had been erased by a grenade, or hurt, or killed by a machine gun's bullet. Never-ending screams and cries covered the noise of the battle, flooding the air like a thunderstorm.

Hundred turned to the left and the right and found

his family safe, but he didn't have time to give his mother a kiss. He pushed them outside, toward the mountains, roughly and rudely, because they didn't want to listen to him. "I cannot come with you, damn it, do as I tell you if you don't want to end up dead!"

To his brother, who was rebelling, he even gave a slap. And finally he saw them leaving across the fields, and he heaved a sigh of relief. He freed himself of the others who were gathering round him as soon as they recognized him, and he rushed toward the house where he had been ordered to go many hours earlier, the house of Mentino and his son, Tanon. He would have liked to have kicked himself for arriving so late.

The house was dark and intact. Hundred knocked on the door, and the door opened as he pushed it in. "They must have run away," he thought. He went inside to see, just to be sure, and he was suddenly very afraid.

"Mentino! Tanon!" he shouted in the darkness of the kitchen. He lit a match. There were Mentino and Tanon, hanging from the grating on the window, with the tips of their toes barely grazing the floor, two centimeters from salvation. And Hundred took them down, shaking, and laid them on the floor. Now he understood everything. The Nazis had killed them before escaping, but it had been the girl who had pointed them out. He had told her the names, those two names that no one else knew.

He sat there a while. From outside the yells and blasts reached his ears, then the din of the tanks and the trucks. It was dawn and there was a great racket in the village. He recognized the song of his comrades:

"The wind is blowing and raising the storm." Here the war was over. Everything was over. The brigade had returned.

So Hundred took his pistol out and released the catch. He wasn't sure if the fault was his or hers. He wasn't sure who should die. Surely someone must. He saw his dead companions out of the corner of his eye, their faces swollen and blue in the gray light of dawn. And even their hands had swollen, and their feet were stretched out straight, trying to reach those last two centimeters they needed to breathe. Hundred put his pistol back in the left side of his jacket. He said to the two motionless figures, "Yes, I have to die. But her too, first."

He went out into the deafening rumble of the Allied tanks, and ran into a group of comrades from the brigade hugging some girls.

"Good for you, Hundred!" they shouted. "Long live Hundred! Come with us, come on and have a drink. You're an ace, the commander's looking for you! . . ."

"I'll be along in a little while," he answered. "Later. Right now I've got something to do."

And he started running desperately in the roar.

Trap Shoot

She was all eyes and brown hair, and they called her Nigrein. She was a *staffetta* in the brigade, continuously biking from one partisan base to another, each scattered among the houses of the peasants in the middle of the countryside. In the nude expanse of plains it was getting more and more difficult to hide, and she passed constantly among Germans and Fascists, crossing roadblocks on the little bridges and at the junctions. And yet the guerrilla war burned everywhere like an invisible fire in a field of brush, and often the enemy realized it only when it was burning the bottoms of its feet.

Nigrein and her entire family were in it up to their necks. The Resistance had begun long before for all of them, with persecution, jail, and confinement. So much so that she and her siblings had grown up like that; it was as if they had suckled the opposition to Fascism together with their mother's milk. They had not been raised with hatred or with arid and vindictive feelings, but they had been taught the simple rules of the earth, about the right to justice and respect for all human persons that, in those grim years under an indifferent tyranny, did not exist.

Small, young, and dark, Nigrein loved her battle name; she had almost forgotten her real name, Adelia, which seemed too bombastic and solemn for her. She liked the little, risky tasks above all, industrious as she was, like an ant that goes up and down, in and out, incessantly, around its safe, excavated little mound of sand, a refuge from the surrounding damp.

In her home, they had already mourned the loss of one of the sons, who had gone off to war in the very beginning and who had never returned. In his place had come a terrible, cold letter, where crests and stamps and official words announced to the family of so-and-so that soldier so-and-so had fallen in battle in a foreign land. Those few, typed lines signed by an indecipherable flourish meant that a strong and thriving young man would never come home again to the house where he was born, nor to the courtyard, nor to the field, nor to the town his eyes had always seen in dreams and memories up to the moment in which they were extinguished.

Nigrein and her family had cried as long as they had tears in them. And then they realized that tears were good for nothing except burning your eyelids and taking your breath away, and that it was better to do honor to their innocent and unprotected dead by fighting a war against the war that had killed him. And they all became partisans, even the youngest son, who was barely fourteen years old. Their home became a base, and each one had his duty. They felt relieved from their pain, entering a new, exciting atmosphere that was consoling even if it did bring dangerous adventures. Time passed quickly like water in a stream that races by, muddy and bright, and it left no opportunity for anguished memories. They were heading toward a solid, concrete limit—not a vendetta, not hatred, but the necessity of liberation, the need for a radical, extreme change, so that it would never again be possible to fall into that irrational and leaden climate of Fascism, in that rotten, devastated world where the war had found the right ground to put down its roots.

The safe spot for Nigrein was her home. It seemed placid and innocuous in the middle of the fields. Her older brother was already off in a brigade. Left behind were her father, the women, and the little boy, too small to be suspect. They continued their work as peasants, taking care of the barn and the animals in the courtyard. They had reaped and tossed the hay and filled the hayloft just like in peacetime. No one could possibly know who was taking refuge there, sleeping in the loft among the armfuls of clover, nor how much stuff was buried jealously under that grassy bed. That was the secret life of the house, guarded by the family, which each day risked death. An imprudent gesture would have been enough, or the cleverness of a Fascist villager, or the mean curiosity of an SS, to set off a disaster. When night fell, the house remained dark and closed in the plains, like a still ship with its lights off and its cargo of weapons and threatened lives.

During an August sunset, four Germans came to the farmhouse. Nigrein saw them from the kitchen window as they crossed the threshing floor of the courtyard, and they saw her, too, her little brown and serious face, and her black eyes and her long, curly hair.

"Bella, ciao, dolce amore!" they said. They were very happy Germans.

"We take cows and bulls," the first one explained, who was a rank officer. "Fast; you open, we take."

The entire family came running; they tried to resist, to persuade them that the animals were necessary to their work, the only defense they had against hunger. But the Germans were firm as rocks, inanimate, with their lips fixed on those few words that they had received as orders: "Us take all animals." Indeed they did take them; they pulled them along by the halters toward the road, and in the meantime they caught sight of the hayloft that was full to overflowing. They spoke amongst themselves and the rank officer added, "We come take grass."

They weren't that happy anymore. They walked away stiff and inflexible, dragging behind themselves the two cows and the two bulls on the rope. The people of the house watched them leave with their last resource, and no one spoke. They knew it was useless. If the Germans got upset, they would have their machine guns sing. Nigrein held her fists to her mouth so as not to scream, and she was crying with rage. As soon as it was night, they had to remove the precious jars of grenades and munitions from the loft and drown them, painfully, into the muddy bottom of the swamp.

After the long summer came another autumn full of fog and storms, and a hard, cold, interminable winter.

The English were resting peacefully in their lodgings along the immobile line of the front. They continued to keep only the fighter-bombers and the reconnaissance prop planes in operation, preparing the burned earth where they would carry out the spring offensive. In that poor land, between the Nazis, who were furious about the defeats on the other fronts, and the Fascists, who little by little were getting drunk with fear, stood the armed partisans and the defenseless population. And every day, in a hundred inhuman ways, the list of the dead grew.

In all that time, Nigrein continued to serve as a *staffetta* for kilometers and kilometers of plains, from house to house, from town to town. Skinny and strong, with her big eyes and her dark hair, her body was still that of a child, but her mind that of an expert partisan. She went along on her bicycle without ever tiring, trembling from the cold and sometimes from terror. But she never would have been able to turn down a mission, because for her, a conscious, live action was infinitely easier and preferable to the heaviness of waiting that wore down the feeble nerves of inactive people.

Spring, indifferent to the matters of the world, put out her swollen buds just in time to give the go-ahead to the late-coming Allies. The partisans of the plains multiplied their actions, ousting the Germans and driving them north. The Fascists began to melt away like snow in the sun. By now, the entire front was moving and the final crush was near. But both Germans and Fascists, in an act of bravado or desperation, each day before leaving, tried to satisfy their own exasperated cruelty. While they were preparing huge suitcases, they didn't forget to flatter the spies. And so it was that a woman, whether paid or by accident, revealed to them the base where the partisan Nappo was hiding along with seven others. They took them at night, surrounding the house. The partisans had just gotten back from a raid that had gone well. They threw themselves down, tired and ready to sleep, and they found the Fascists on top of them. Unarmed, hit, beaten, and kicked, they were tied up with wide ropes and could not free themselves. And so began their transfer march to who knows where.

Nappo was the battle name of Nigrein's brother.

Onward, onward, under the guns of the Fascists. Onward in a light, tepid, April rain, without knowing the places where they were being dragged. The Fascists laughed and insulted them, or they asked for the names of other partisans and information about bases and plans. Confronted with the partisans' hard and indignant silence, they often became furious and beat them. Just like that, stupidly. Now a sudden backhand against the mouth, now a push, now a kick with their big military shoes. The eight partisans were quiet and quivering in front of the black holes of the submachine guns, which were always pointed at their backs. Across deserted secondary streets they came to a small, unknown town and they were locked in barracks. They were wet and sweaty, dirty with blood. Other soldiers replaced the ones who had accompanied them. And so they began anew with fresh force to beat the prisoners.

A rosy dawn came up that their eyes, swollen closed,

did not see. Through their beaten, split, bloodied lips only laments had passed, and few even of those. Only when the pain expanded in waves—surprisingly acute like a needle or somber like a boulder, along the length of their bodies, from their feet to their necks—then they emitted moans. Or they were silent, even under the fiercest blows. Not a word, not an intelligible syllable did the Fascists obtain with their exhausting rage. In the end they got tired, tied the partisans up with wire, and threw them down on the floor in a big room, separated from one another, in the dark.

They came to, little by little, although they could not move. The metal wire was tight and it cut the skin. They called to each other softly, and heard that they were all still alive, although in terrible pain.

"What will they do to us?" asked Pin, who was very young.

"My feet hurt," complained another.

"They're there behind that door," a voice from the back said—it was Nappo. "I hear them. They are listening to see if we say anything."

"That'll be the day!" laughed Ilarino bitterly. He was the oldest one, but right away he moaned with pain.

They looked around themselves, moving their heads with great difficulty. But they could see nothing; every opening to the room was blocked, and they understood only from the sound of their own voices that the room must be very big. They were quiet and motionless because every gesture brought pain. They tried to recuperate their strength in the silence, and finally, worn out, they dozed off.

They were awakened with a start by someone who had entered like a wolf. Two Fascists with a muted flashlight were going from man to man cutting the wire bonds with pliers. They were working hard between the wire and the flesh, and they cast insults and curses at each other. No one answered; no one complained. They clenched their teeth in the suffering of reopened wounds; they tried slowly to stretch their arms and legs, to reacquire the use of their limbs and easy movement. But one of the Fascists kept an eye on them with his machine gun while the other one broke the last knots.

"On your feet," the first one ordered, holding his loaded firearm against his thigh. They were pushed forward in a tight group, leaning against one another, and then they suddenly turned off the flashlights.

"Outside," a voice shouted, and a big door opened wide against the light of morning, on the countryside washed by the rain. The partisans ran toward the light, dazzled like pigeons that are freed from closed cages as they take to the sky in a shooting range.

A multitude of shots rang out, and they fell one by one, face down on the cement of the courtyard, with their arms open on the grass of the lane or on the thorns of the hedge. All of them except Pin, who careened around the corner of the house and disappeared behind the vines, gaining the speed of a rocket in his desperate will to live. Maybe the Fascists didn't notice it, or maybe they no longer cared about running after him. They knew that after such a massacre there was no time to lose. Even their own lives now depended on the quickness of escape.

Nigrein was on a truck in the middle of the partisans in the center of town. They were yelling and singing with joy for the liberation. The flags were raised in the blue air. It was finally that long-awaited day, the day they had dreamed of, and for which they had paid dearly. She looked around in the crowd and was sure that she would soon see here or there the face of her brother Walter, who had taken Nappo as his battle name. She was laughing and seemed fuller, prettier, with her long hair and her shining eyes. She heard a partisan call insistently, calling from the street below, "Come! We have to go get the bodies. We have to prepare the funerals. They can't stay down there. They killed seven of them. Only Pin made it out alive. But Ilarino is dead, and Zigzag, . . . and Nappo."

Nigrein didn't understand at first; it was as if a fog had invaded her. At last the words penetrated her like needles, and she jumped down from the truck. The entire happy, tumultuous scene became motionless in her eyes.

"They killed Walter," she screamed, without tears. She ran away, toward her home, toward her unknowing mother. Running behind her was the partisan who unknowingly had brought her the word of death. He called her loudly by name. And he was crying.

The Commander

Bruno started shaking off the veils of fear after he left the factory and attached the first little poster to a column of the portico at night. He was hiding with the other comrades in the basements of the bombed-out houses on the outskirts of town. As soon as night fell, they went through the city with a jar of glue under one arm, quiet and quick as cats. If they heard a step or a noise, they hid, scattering among the piles of rubble or throwing themselves into unhinged doorways. Here they waited, immobile, listening to the hollow beating of their hearts.

This lasted until the day they left for the mountain. They had to leave almost without saying good-bye. They came out of those black holes of the basements, one going one way, another going another, by now having decided to resist, even if the undertaking seemed to be stronger than they were.

At the last minute, they thought they'd never see each other again.

Bruno came to the brigade one sky blue morning in winter. The light and the cold put a burning sensation of pungent tears in his eyes. But he felt full of a naked, calm happiness, without memories of home, without feeling sorry about anything, not even his mother, who had been left all alone. He understood that it had to be this way, if he was going to become good at anything. He found himself in the midst of comrades who were tall, big, tan. He was neither very tall, nor big, and he seemed younger than his years. He was ashamed of his white, city face, whiter still for the long hours spent underground. But soon he got color in the sun, in the crude air. He had never left the plains, but he quickly got used to the woods, the slopes, the rocks, the lying in wait, the action. He liked climbing up a summit and looking down at the path that he had taken to get there.

He wasn't one of those who volunteered for risky adventures, but he went where he was sent, and he was never tired before the others. He was only jealous of those who had a better musket than his own, which was quite nice and clean; he kept it with extreme diligence.

The commander became for him the dearest and most feared person—a human, living representation of his own partisan passion. Now instead of looking for courage in his heart, he looked for it there, in that gray man with the red face and an almost constant smile in his light blue eyes, small in the hard wrinkles. Those eyes intimidated him, but he learned to stare at them without turning his head away, even if he almost felt the need to do so. He knew that the commander had been a *Garabaldino* in Spain, and it was obvious he was afraid of nothing.

In the days nearest to death, certain orders of the

commander's seemed really incomprehensible, even though Bruno did not find the means to question them, not even in his deepest self. Those orders were resolved in a clear proof of ability, of competence. The commander was the first one to advance and the last to retreat. When they were in a calm period, everyone liked seeing the short, peaceful smoke of his pipe, a pipe that was filled maybe only with dry grass in order that the partisans of the formation, using the big papers bought on the black market and the tobacco that had been saved, could have their cigarettes.

It was his commander who gave him his battle name, Little Boy, the first day, certainly due to his delicate and young face. And Little Boy it stayed, even when he aged in the months on the mountainside. He learned to understand that man well, a man who was responsible not only for their lives, but even for a part, big or small that it may be, of the partisan war. Not only him, but all the comrades had come to know the commander, little by little, as they came to the brigade. His countenance was among them, each day a little more open and intelligible, and they read him like a newspaper. On the desperate mountain, in the sun and in the snow, his look that was neither indulgent nor tender, but able and conscious; it was as necessary as bread, as arms. It represented the certainty of freeing oneself from the war, from the desire to kill the enemy—to free oneself through fighting, without hatred, but for necessity.

The day that they left, he said good-bye with his hand, simply, saying "Good-bye, boys." He left on a jeep, with his pipe in his mouth, this time filled with good tobacco. Everyone was laughing and screaming because the war was over, everyone was going home. And yet they were sorry to see that jeep start off, and it seemed impossible that there could be disappointment in a day like that.

Bruno came home late that night. The city was happy, filled with Allied soldiers—English, Polish, Americans, and Negroes—arm and arm with the girls. He looked around and it almost seemed he couldn't recognize the streets. They seemed geometric to him, transparent, amazing, like those you see in a dream. His own street, small and out of the way, was dark and quiet, and looked more like when he'd left it, convincing him that indeed he was living in reality. He rang the doorbell and the house filled with voices. He met the hugs, the tears, the smell of his mother.

He was sorry to miss the day of liberation. It had been the twenty-first of April, four days earlier. They all told him about it, what a great thing it had been, the immense joy, the enthusiasm! Each person told the story in his or her own way, but everyone who had lived that day had shouted in the streets, hugging partisans, English, Polish, Negroes. For him, on the other hand, the liberation had been the last battle, and he had seen his comrades die; he had shot all the ammo in his Sten. And then they'd said good-bye. "So long, boys!" the commander had said from his jeep. And each one had gone down the mountain late, each on his own.

He realized right away he was living in a strange world, even if he was itching for news of the insurrection in the cities of the north, for the disorderly escape of the enemy, for the execution of the criminals, Mussolini and his men. There existed, even here near him, groups of people with no memory. The persecution, the round-ups, the tortures, those slaughtered in the streets, the scared savagery of the Nazis, the merciless cowardice of the Fascists; all of this was vague and lost. For many, the war had passed like clear water, and now they shook themselves off a bit and found themselves once again dry. Bruno listened to them talk with passion about things that had no importance, and he had the curious sensation of being in a foreign country where he only partially understood the language. Someone who knew him said, "Tell the truth: It would have been better if you'd stayed home. The war would have ended anyway."

And he saw in a flash the faces of his dead companions, those who had died fighting, and he went away quickly so as not to punch the man out.

He wandered around the street among the new uniforms of the Allies and the girls' bare arms, occasionally entering a café. But he could still see the mountain: the marches, the cold, the assaults, the sun, the fear—yes, even the fear—and everything came back to him in the present, a living memory, a life that didn't end. Even when he took one of those girls by the bare arm and took her for a walk on the hills. She would say to him, "Nice partisan!" like she would have said any other thing, and he held her in his arms, kissing her, begging her to be quiet.

It was exactly on the return from one of these amorous walks, at the city gates, that it happened. He met a red face, he saw the gray hair, the sky blue eyes in the little wrinkles.

"How are you, Little Boy?" the commander said. "Good for you," he indicated the girl on his arm, adding, "Is this your fiancée?"

The partisan felt himself slip into a cloud of memories and he felt himself tied by a new bondage, one that he had never felt even during the hardest days on the mountain.

"Commander!" he said. "My commander!"

The girl watched them both, waiting.

"We're back now," said the red and gray man. "No more commander, now, only comrade. Come, let's get a coffee together."

They were in a piazza filled with rubble. The bombings had always hit this area, even if it wasn't that close to the railways. In a shed leaning against a wall that was still standing, there was a bar with an espresso machine, a few tables and chairs outside. "Let's sit," the commander said. Before the cups of coffee, as the girl, lost in thought, was stirring the sugar, the gray man said, "I know what you're thinking. I've seen others like you. It's not everything that we expected. But we can keep our responsibility. Remember, the responsibility like we had on the mountain."

He looked up with his little, light eyes, like when he

would scan the summits. "We still have to be ready to fight against the war. Even as grown-ups. Get it, Little Boy?"

He started laughing a sweet laugh, and he made a gesture of a caress toward the girl's hair, without touching it.

"Well, well," he said with conviction. "You have found yourself a good-looking little girl."

Acquitted

The child Vincenzo left school with his friends. They rushed down the three little stairs jumping, as if the main door had violently thrown them out of the building when it swung open widely. They scattered, fanning out across the courtyard, screaming, the kind of flooding torrent that breaks dams.

"Mario, Marioooo!" Vincenzo shouted, and he ran behind a boy who was leaving quickly on his own with his coat all crooked and slung over one shoulder. "Speak, bullfighter!" He was hot on his heels, pulling up alongside, and the other boy turned a small, sharp face, bitter as a lemon. "What do you want? You know I'm in a rush."

"I wanted to ask if you still have the little figures from the Torino team," Vincenzo said. "They told me you wanted to sell them."

This story is autobiographical. Antonio Meluschi, the author's husband, was really arrested in 1949, like hundreds of other partisans subjected to persecution. Police, *carabinieri,* and a judicial branch composed of almost completely the same men who had made their careers under Fascism arrested, imprisoned, and slandered those who had fought to free the country from the Fascists and the Germans, to alleviate the conditions at the moment of the peace accord.

"Who would be so crazy?" Mario bawled, hoarsely. "You need some real money for the entire team. They're rare now!"

"But I," Vincenzo insisted, "have a photo portrait of all the dead ones, including the journalists and the coaches. The entire plane that went down."*

"Pufff!" went Mario, disdainfully. Skipping along two or three steps, he slipped his arm into his overcoat and fumbled around for the other sleeve. In the meantime, he glanced sideways to see if Vincenzo was following him.

"Where is this portrait, anyway?" he asked with his usual rude tone.

"At home," Vincenzo replied. "Really beautiful. There are photos of all their faces around the border of the picture. In the center is the date of their death, the years they won the championship, the emblem of the Torino team, and lots of other things. You should really see it! My mother bought it for me Sunday, when we went to the game."

A sense of profound commiseration appeared in Mario's glance, sharp as a tack. "Of course, because you, at twelve years old, still go to the game with mommy!"

"She doesn't want me to go alone," Vincenzo admitted, weakly. "But my mother is really a sport," he added,

* In 1949, a plane carrying the entire Juventus team (the soccer team of Turin, and one of the most famous and best teams in Italy) crashed at Superga, near Turin, killing all aboard.

recovering himself. "She's a writer and she knows a lot about everything."

"A writer!" Mario said. "Humph!"

The subject didn't interest him, so he changed it quickly.

"The little figures are better, anyway, and they're not making them anymore, from now on. By now . . . today is December 6. They died in May, the Torino team, so it's been . . ." He started to count on his fingers, "seven months."

"Exactly, and that's why the portrait is better," Vincenzo asserted. "And it's done with real photographs, only their heads. It's supposed to be framed, as a souvenir. You used to play with the little figures, but now how can you?"

They had stopped between two columns of the portico. The fog stung them and soaked them like rain. And even Vincenzo's sweet face, a little bit surprised, was strewn with cold little drops. He wiped them away with a wet sleeve of his coat. "Do as you wish," he said. "I can go get the picture to show it to you. Then, if you like it, you can give me the figures. By the way, have you ever been to the stadium?"

They stared at each other, as if oppressed and bound by that precise, almost aggressive question, that begged a precise answer.

"No," Mario confessed, unsure about his own ability to sustain a lie so easily proven with evidence. "But if I go, I'll go alone."

"Wait for me here," Vincenzo said, with condescending pity. "My father is home. My mother is in Calabria, on a trip to write some articles for the newspaper."

"And your father, what does he do in the meantime?" Mario asked, freshly spiteful and full of revenge. "The housework?"

Vincenzo, who had already taken off running, did a complete about-face. "My father is also a writer, and what's more, he's a partisan commander!"

Mario hid his ignorance quickly behind a barrier of suspicious indifference. "Puffff!"

But the other was not listening to him, he ran along the street, headed towards home, his little gray house that was still standing as if forgotten among the ruins of the huge buildings destroyed in the bombings. He rang the bell three times at the small front door. An opaque silence hung around him, a fragmented landscape in the fog. He pushed the button, keeping his thumb bent, the trill dying on the inside, pushed aside by the emptiness. Someone rang him in, but the door at the top of the first flight of stairs did not open. From the top somewhere a woman's voice called "Vincenzo!" and the child ran quickly up the steps, giving his closed, mute door a big hit as he passed it. He went up to the second floor. The neighbor was on the landing and told him as he was coming up, "Your dad went off with two of his friends. He said that you should go right away to Annie's house."

"Off?" Vincenzo murmured. "Off where?"

"I don't know," the neighbor said. "He had to go. They were all in a big hurry. Do you know where Annie lives? Do you know her?"

Vincenzo replied, "Yes, I know."

A big chill took him there on the dark stairs, on the landing of his house where a golden blade of light extended outward, where his mom and dad opened the door right away, having already heard his whistles and shouts from the street below. He knocked again once, even if he knew it was useless, and then he went down again slowly, finding himself once again outside and alone. It was lunchtime, and there was no one going by on the street. The stores had their lights on because of the fog, but by now they were pulling the shutters closed and closing the windows. The rubble made the passage narrow among the surviving houses. At the end of the street, at the corner, he spied the small figure of Mario, waiting, and he ran toward him but did not stop.

"So where is this famous picture?" he shouted impatiently.

Vincenzo passed him running. "It's not there. It's not there anymore. There's nobody there anymore."

Only the fear that Mario might overtake him kept him from crying.

Enrica got off the train in Bologna after twenty-two hours of travel. The excitement had taken root, and she felt immersed in an unreal atmosphere. For one night and one day she had watched the colors, panoramas, and climates change, from the warm air of spring in Crotone, to the soft gray sky of Rome, to the sparkling snows on the backs of the Apennines. She had managed to eat and sleep a little, quick naps suspended in the noise of the train's wheels. She woke suddenly; she felt as if she'd slept a long time, but it had only been twenty minutes, a quarter of an hour. She had even conversed with some people in the compartment, light, superficial conversations, train subjects; but she would never have been able to remember either the faces or the words.

Every so often she would look at the telegram again without reading it, and then she knew with certainty that her husband had been arrested. "I'm at Portomaggiore," the telegram said. "Child alone stop come home right away stop. Gianni." No one was sick nor had other things happened. In prison. Gianni was in prison. Otherwise how could he be in Portomaggiore, the big town near the valleys where he had commanded his partisan brigade? And "come home right away," when he knew these articles about Calabria were important—the investigation about the massacre of Melissa, three dead and twenty wounded, the police bearing arms against citizens, against the occupation of the land. Her first journalistic feature story, accepted with great commitment and responsibility.

She remembered how she had left Bologna a few days earlier, at night. While happy to be going, in that last moment she had certainly suffered a bit on the train as it moved away. Behind her, in the lights of the tracks, she was leaving her two family members, her husband and her child, who had accompanied her to the train. She was detaching herself from them, erasing them, one tall and one small, as they held hands. And now, "child alone" the telegram said. "Here we are," thought Enrica, as she placed her feet almost uncer-

tainly on the firm ground after so much motion. "It's
here that I said good-bye to them."

The transparent, fictional calm that she had tried
desperately to maintain was evaporating; but as fragile
as it was, she needed it. She slipped to the bottom of
her anxiety, walking along the wide, cold curve of the
underpass, expansive and bright like in a dream, a few
people scattered randomly here and there, who seemed
to be hanging onto their suitcases, as she was. And she
was seized again by a sense of unreality, until she could
breathe better again, coming up onto that piazza en-
gulfed by fog, with the weight of the low rain hanging in
the air. She gave the address to the taxi and he got there
in a few minutes, crossing wide streets that were already
dark and big areas reflecting the golden light of street-
lamps and shopwindows. The small house among the
ruins was mute and closed; she saw it with the same eyes
as Vincenzo had the day before. The place seemed new,
distant, unrecognizable, a doorbell that rang in the
emptiness. But she at least knew that no one was there.
And while she rang the bell out of habit, she was already
looking for her keys in her purse. She opened the door,
reached the door at the top of the stairs, and went into
the abandoned smell of her own rooms.

In that moment she felt she had brutally run into a
reality she didn't deserve, a real danger, an injustice
that operated without regard against her husband, her
son—a child!—and against herself. She saw herself at
the beginning of an unknown road, the object of a hate
that wounded her, perhaps even mortally, her and all
the other innocents. There was an offensive against the

partisans; the Resistance was on trial, the Resistance that was something that had been going on for quite some time, but in which she hadn't even believed that much. She believed in it now, desperately, and she had direct knowledge of it. And it was, besides her anguish, a terrible disappointment, the loss of an extreme value that left her at once afraid and impoverished.

It was a weak passageway over a violent river that didn't last. All the moments of the partisan war returned to her memory: she remembered her own courage, that courage in wartime that she didn't have at first and that she had constructed for herself, so as not to be confused and inefficient. She recovered that courage from her past, together with a shot of anger, of rebellion, of disdain, that reassured her. She knew she would not cry or beg anyone. Only with her rights clear in her mind could she go forward. She angrily dried the insubordinate tears that burned her face. When she opened the drawers and saw the small clothes of her child, she grabbed a few things and some of his schoolbooks, made a bundle, and left.

The woman from the second floor told her that two men had come to get Mr. Gianni. They had come up to their apartment, and Mr. Gianni had said, "When you see my son, send him to Annie's! I have to go away with these two friends." Just like that, nothing else. She had the impression they weren't really friends. They were silent and kept close to his side. Going down, one was in front and the other in back.

"They were policemen," Enrica said. "They arrested him. Thank you, and excuse me."

She ran down the stairs but then realized she had not been very nice to that helpful woman, who had at least sent the child to a safe place. She also knew that she was good and that she could trust her. From the ground floor she shouted loudly, "Excuse me again, and thank you from the heart, Signora Maria!"

In the street, with her bag and her small suitcase, in the devastated landscape, it felt like six or seven years earlier, when she was still carrying revolvers and explosives in her shopping bag.

She found Vincenzo at Annie's house, calm and serene. Everyone had experienced this particular quality of hers, when she had been a partisan in the valleys. Annie was reassuring; any moment could become a rest break. She didn't have to overcome fear with courage: for her it simply didn't exist, and even danger had no meaning for her. Her German origins had left her a rigorous, controlled rationality and a unique, foreign pronunciation that was both rough and sweet. She loved her Italian family; she felt she had nothing in common anymore with her country of provenance, if not the loving sorrow for her dead parents. In her every act or commitment she was clear, passionate, impeccable. She was like a solid tree planted in the middle of a flowering bush.

Enrica hugged the child and told him about his father's arrest. She was used to talking to him freely about serious, weighty things, as if speaking to a man. She told Annie she was going to see Gianni. "I'll leave Vincenzo with you," she added with an immense relief, putting down her worries about her son like a heavy bundle. She had revived in that warm and attentive presence. She ate something very quickly, having suddenly realized that she was dying of hunger. And she ran off; as soon as she was outside, she was hit by a driving rain.

At the newspaper, they knew nothing. In the usual noisy confusion of nighttime excitement, the news of Gianni's arrest hit like a ton of bricks, and his name was on everyone's lips. An editor ran down to the *carabinieri* headquarters and to the police headquarters. He found himself in the midst of strange looks and small gestures with heads, or dark and uncomprehending faces. He was sent from one office to another. He even spoke with the big cheeses: A high-ranking officer. A state official.

"We have no record of this," said the high-ranking officer of the *carabinieri*. "We have no record of this," affirmed the state official at police headquarters. Gianni, after the very brief passage by the neighbor's house and the mysterious telegram, had disappeared into nothingness.

"Let's go to Portomaggiore," Enrica said. A painful, hot flash passed through her blood suddenly, from her head to her toes. "We're not even sure he's in the hands of the police."

It was ten o'clock at night, and it was still raining.

"Go on," the editor-in-chief said. "You and Piero from the local news and the driver, Dado. Be careful; there's flooding near Ferrara."

Enrica curled up in a corner of the car, and Piero tried to make her as comfortable as possible. It wasn't a beautiful car, it was used only for transporting the newspapers. The roof was little more than a waterproof canvas, and the water came in on both sides. Soon there was a puddle on the floor, and Dado threw an old rag on top of it without so much as stopping. Dado had been a partisan, and he wasn't easily disturbed. Even with regard to Gianni, he was optimistic.

"I'm full of rags—I keep a warehouse full because the windshield wipers break often and I have to dry the windshield myself."

On the wet asphalt, the headlights cast an intrepid, if slightly tremulous, light. The left one missed a beat every so often, as if it were almost winking.

"It's not a car that could do the Mille Miglia, certainly," said Dado. "But it goes fast. Are you afraid, Enrica?"†

"With you, I'd go to the North Pole," she answered. And with that breath of good humor, something was born between them that annihilated the dim, indistinct thoughts and the sad light of premonition in the traveling companions, in their movements, in their actions.

"Certainly it's better to do anything rather than sit and wait," Piero added softly. "Even if it is a bit cold out."

The countryside was immense and dark. They could hear from far away a dull, tenacious roar. It was a recognizable sound, similar to that of many running motors, or to a waterfall.

"It sounds like the noise of the front," Enrica observed, who once again felt catapulted into the past.

---

† The Mille Miglia is a road race, comparable to the Indianapolis 500.

"It's the flood," Dado declared placidly. "Have no fear; we're going in a different direction."

They got tired during the long kilometers. They were now in a dead and silent world, with bare drawings of trees that escaped behind them, with the houses like dark spots. The rain was diminishing and the ice was increasing in the weak light of the night. They no longer felt like talking, and Dado, intent on the driving, hummed and whistled to keep himself awake. They were experiencing the useless restlessness of hopelessly wanting warm rooms and boiling beverages, of taking off their cold clothes and of drying their faces with a big, clean towel. The town on the plains seemed to come upon them, with its tightly nestled houses, the tall streetlights, a piazza, a church, a building.

"Portomaggiore! We're here," announced Dado. "There's the *carabinieri* barracks."

The rain picked up again in that moment, furiously.

"Stay in the car," Enrica said. "It's more likely they'll open up for me if I'm alone."

As soon as she was under the short recess of the barred front door, she rang the bell. Nothing and no one. An abandoned city. She continued to turn the old doorbell. She heard the ring in the distance, as if suffocated, and she heard a heavy step that seemed to be coming down a long stairway with difficulty. Someone invisible opened a little window and with a strong voice asked, "Who is it?" There was no response to her quick, clear answer, and the little window closed.

With her ear to the door against the wood, in the

noisy rush of a broken gutter, Enrica heard another step and again the little window opened.

"Nothing. It's forbidden," said another voice. Enrica tried to push a hand in the opening. "Excuse me. I come from Bologna. I am looking for my husband. I want to see him, I'm not asking for anything. Tell me only if he is here."

Silence.

"We need the Signor Capitano," the voice answered. She was invaded by the intense passion of life, determined. She took her hand away; one word was enough for her.

"Call him, please!" She was like a runner about to cross the finish line.

"The Signor Captain is sleeping," the voice pronounced, detached, definitive. "He doesn't want to be awakened."

They returned. The clamor of the rain had extended everywhere. It seemed to fill the landscape, blocking the emptiness of the sky with great, rustling curtains. It accompanied the motor like a musical background, but monotonous and sleep-inducing. All of a sudden something changed in the vast waves of sounds. It was a small, weak shot, and the windshield wipers stopped. "I knew it," said Dado simply, pulling out his bundle of rags. They were going slowly now, almost immersed in a sea of fog. Every so often they stopped, and the men took turns getting out to clean the outside of the windshield. Enrica was in her corner, not moving. She was

no longer cold or tired and had no desire to do anything. She was suspended in that rocking, thrown back
and forth with the bounces of the car. She asked herself
vaguely where they were going and if they would ever
arrive anywhere. She was sorry she had brought Piero
and Dado into that adventure, but it was a superficial
sorriness, just a quick thought, like an annoyance, a
bother. She heard their voices, excited, cursing; she
would have liked to excuse herself for creating such a
fuss, but she decided not to, out of laziness. Maybe she
was about to fall asleep. Instead she jumped up with a
violent reaction, gaining back her readiness and her
will. She fought with herself to be able to fight the fatigue and the dark, stormy night like the others. From
the windows she saw a gray, thick, immobile expanse,
and she recognized the place, a riverbank that she had
walked many times during the clandestine war.

"It's the water, it's the water, Dado!" she shouted.

They got out; she hadn't been deceived. The front
wheels were already touching the edge of the levee.
What lay beyond, what seemed to be solid ground, was
the water of the flood that had filled the field and
reached the road.

"Good God," said Dado. It seemed that his strong
hands sustained and brought the weight of the car back
onto the sure road. A warm rush of happiness touched
the three of them, and they started to laugh, in a
friendly way.

"How did you manage to see that, you who can't see
beyond the end of your nose?" Dado asked. "I mean, no
offense—"

"But it's absolutely true that I'm as blind as a bat! No offense taken!" Enrica replied. "It must be that I've passed by here before, or I was able to see with the eyes of fear!"

They left again. The last kilometers were the best. It was raining lightly and the ice let up in the white unraveling of the fog. Inside the wet car, with soaking gloves, they had trouble lighting their cigarettes. Enrica was amazed she was hungrier than she was tired.

"It's that you sleep with your stomach and you eat with your bed," Dado explained. When he'd been in action, whatever it was, he felt nothing. They got back to the newspaper at four in the morning, the darkest hour in winter. The newsroom was awake, warm and crowded. They had waited for them all night, to get the news into the city edition at least. But there was no news, except that a partisan commander, a writer and journalist, had been arrested two days earlier. Why, how, where he was, they did not know.

Enrica slept dressed, with the light on. She lay down like that, as soon as she entered the house, thinking she'd rest a moment, but she fell deeply asleep, as if into a well. She dreamed she was still in Calabria, under a strange, yellow sky. She had her child by the hand, but he was small, one or two years old. She saw him with his face from then, a round, sweet face, the eyes always turned up toward her, asking something, big eyes that were a sweet brown color with the whites almost blue. She didn't know why she was in Calabria with the small child, nor if it was really Calabria. She asked herself how she would get back home, clinging as she was to a rocky outcropping, that then became a building of many floors. She stepped back so as not to fall, but her legs were two rolls of stuffing. She couldn't move them. The child was no longer there; who knows where she'd lost him. With a huge effort she started to call him and the scream woke her. Trembling, she returned to her life, suddenly finding her lucid anguish. A cloudy morning was barely brightening the windows, and the room was pale and icy, like a dead person.

But Enrica was alive, and mounting in her again was the heat of rage. She no longer had any tender thought about the suffering of her husband, nor did she suffer like a woman for her man. She felt herself strong, as strong as he, who certainly would not let himself be beaten. She knew him too well; she knew everything about him as if she'd created him herself, like her son. Gianni had been in prison under Fascism, and he had come out of it more solid than ever. All their common existence had been made up of waiting, of clandestine action, of hopes cultivated like flowers in the hard days, hopes that had become ever more open and ambitious: bushes, trees, forests of hopes. And they had become certainties in war, when they moved toward liberation. She had never been sorry for that time, even if it had been full of risk and fear. She would not have wanted to remain with the child in a safe place, waiting for her companion. Nor would she have been happy if her companion, after all that they had dreamed and prepared for, had remained behind with her to wait. They had never spoken heavy words. Just, "Let's go. And we'll take the child with us." And they had been in the partisan war for nineteen months.

Now, sure of her husband, she didn't fear for herself. She had absolutely no reason to change her sense of him—honest, loyal, innocent. She was indignant only for the attack on liberty, on a man's rights. She was filled with anger for the insidious arrest, surreptitious, as if he were a criminal. She considered herself a victim of a moral outrage, for the state of anxiety in which they kept her. You've taken Gianni, she thought, by error or by calumny. Fine. Say so: so-and-so is in such-and-such a place, accused of this and that. But don't take him away from his home, leaving a child in the street, and refuse to tell his wife that you even know whether or not he is in police custody. At this point something painful shook her, as if she had dragged a rough hand across a wound. "But is it really true he's in police custody?"

She went out into the clear and freezing morning. The long rain had washed the asphalt, and the ice had dried it as if in a summer sun. The city was hard, sonorous, clean, and Enrica had her usual look, like an even-tempered woman, no longer young but pleasant and healthy. She went directly to police headquarters and asked to speak in person to the chief of police. This time it went better; they had her come in right away and she met with a capable man. One who knew Gianni and herself as writers and who had had a partisan son. "Here we have no record of it," he said, with great gentleness. Enrica pronounced then all the words of her heart: she was neither rude nor aggressive. Defense moved in her like an instinct. "I'd better be good, or they'll put me in prison," and she checked her sentences for their politeness. But there was ardor in her voice, in her wringing hands, in her tearless eyes; the tension dried her face like a parched land. She seemed much older but she did not plead. She did not speak of her own pain, nor did she seek pity for her child. She knew what she wanted to say, syllable by syllable.

"But if your husband is in Portomaggiore, the case would be under Ferrara's jurisdiction," said the police chief quietly. Enrica reddened like a child caught eating the sugar. It's true, it's true! Why didn't they think of it, she and her colleagues from the newspaper?

"I'm not experienced in these things," she said. "Excuse me. I'll go right away to Ferrara. Would you do me the favor of telephoning ahead so they receive me? Thank you."

She shook the extended hand and ran away. While she was waiting to leave, in a garage of rental cars, she felt herself bursting with joy. "If they'd only told me, the *carabiniere* of the small window!" she thought, almost forgetting the long night, the rain, the flood, the cold, the fear. "If only they had said, yes, he's here."

In Ferrara it wasn't easy either. The screws, loosened for a moment, started to turn and tighten again. First off, Enrica arrived at two in the afternoon, and at the police station they told her to come back later. They weren't even certain that she would be received.

"The police chief of Bologna has sent me," she affirmed. "He's already telephoned the chief here." They all started laughing.

"The Signor police chief," said one in uniform, "has received no telephone call."

"We'll see about that," Enrica exclaimed, her face in flames.

She forced herself to pass the time without making herself nervous. She ate lunch in a small, deserted restaurant where they served her reluctantly because the lunch hour had passed. She walked slowly under the porticoes, remembering other, happier stops in that city. She shook her head so that the revived memories would not bring tears to her eyes. She drank two coffees, scolding herself for having done it. She thought of sending a postcard to Vincenzo; then she no longer felt like it. At four o'clock she went back up the stairs of the police headquarters. She found the officers much nicer; obviously the phone call had come in.

"Your husband is in Portomaggiore, it's certain," the chief told her, with a sober greeting and an inexpressive face, when she reached his ample desk after crossing many rooms. "But don't complain, eh? He is being treated with great respect. I spoke this very minute with the Captain. Your husband was stopped."

"I'm not complaining," Enrica murmured, still strictly controlling herself. "But tell me why . . ."

"This, I don't know, ma'am," said the official. And he got up.

"While we're speaking," he added, "your husband is in the office of the Captain. It's heated, you know . . ."

The interview was over, with a shadow of a smile that bounced from face to face of the agents to the last one at the door. "Good luck," Enrica told herself as she got back in the car, and she told the chauffeur to drive quickly to Portomaggiore.

In the light of day, the barracks had a less sinister look, and she stared at it benevolently thinking Gianni was inside there, in the warmth of the Captain's office.

"Maybe your husband will come home with us," said the driver, now abreast of the situation, in solidarity.

"Yes. No. Well, maybe not," Enrica said, defending herself from that spark of hope. She rang the bell and the door opened right away without further ado.

"Make yourself comfortable," said the *carabiniere*. "The Signor Captain is waiting for you."

The office was illuminated by powerful lights, and the Captain came toward her, polished and smooth in his uniform. The very first thing Enrica saw was the radiator.

"Are you Mrs. R.?" the Captain said. "Good. Tell me how you found out your husband was here? You were expecting his arrest, perhaps?"

He was big and large; he dominated her from on high. The charge of anguish and anger returned to overwhelm Enrica, but she managed to contain it. She became red, maybe also for the blaze of the fire.

"I'm sorry," she pronounced with a frank and exact voice. "We were not waiting for anything. Nor did we have any reason to. I was in Calabria, my husband was taken away, and my son was left locked out of the house, alone."

"And so?" the Captain said.

"And so I received a telegram," Enrica declared. She

took it out of her pocketbook and placed it down, the yellow sheet trembling slightly in her hand.

"So he," said the Captain, "was expecting to be taken at any moment."

"But can't you see that it was sent when Gianni was already in your hands? Have the patience to look at the hour." Enrica's voice had grown in tone but was still steady and measured.

The Captain examined the yellow paper. "It's not possible."

"How can that be, it's not possible?" Enrica exclaimed. "My husband found an understanding, nice person among the *carabinieri,* and that's it! One who understood the case and let him send the telegram."

"We'll see about that," said the Captain, and he went to sit down at his desk.

Enrica started to regret her words. She had been insolent. Maybe she had done harm to some poor devil. She wanted to make it up in some way. "Captain," she said in a small voice. "Please excuse me. I've been looking for my husband since the day before yesterday, day and night. Now I'm reassured knowing that he is here. Maybe there's been a mistake, but I'm not blaming anyone. If you would let me see him a moment, please. Only to let him know that the child and I are fine. Anyway, the arrest will be revoked; it may expire. Today, . . . I don't know . . . maybe tomorrow he'll be able to come home . . ."

"I'm very sorry, ma'am" said the Captain slowly. "Your husband is no longer here. Just a little while before your arrival here, he was transferred to the prisons of Ravenna, and the detention was converted to an arrest."

This time Enrica started to cry.

Gianni was handed over to the judicial authorities for possession of arms and conspiracy to subvert the powers of the State. After four months in prison, he was acquitted for not having committed the crime. Those were the years in which the partisans paid dearly for the privilege of having fought and suffered for freedom.

My Resistance

I wrote *L'Agnese va a morire* as a novel, but I invented none of it. It is my war testimony. It is the reason why the Resistance is still for me the most important of all the things I've done in my life. I lived it before writing it, and I didn't realize I was living in the thick of it, day after day. The character of Agnese is not just one person. I never met a woman named Agnese who did the things I said she did. But many "Agneses" were with me in the deeds and events of the war. And the events and deeds either really happened, and so close by that I was sure of their truth, or were such that I directly participated in them, sometimes without even knowing it at that moment and only realizing it later. Agnese is the synthesis, the representation of all the women who left a simple, defined life of hard work and a poor family, to go beyond their limited scope, opening their minds and leaving behind the small things, finding themselves among the crowd that was building the path to freedom. If it had not been for them, the women, the partisan army would have lost a vital, necessary force.

Renata Viganò had recently written these autobiographical pages published in the volume *La Resistenza a Bologna*. Born in Bologna in 1900, the author died there April 23, 1976.

Women—the women workers, day laborers, peasants from the plains and the mountains—got used to "men's business" and little by little understood, each one according to her own level of intelligence, with courage and with fear, that *this* was the thing to do. And so they were a determinative force. A working-class woman is a fighter, when she fights for herself and her people, if it's against poverty in peacetime, or if it's for life in wartime. The partisan war was not an abominable war like one of conquest, but one that was accepted and fought to beat the enemies of all time: oppressors in the homeland and foreign aggressors.

I was not born working class. Therefore I did not have the great lesson of a hard childhood, of parents who were exhausted by difficult jobs, by daily deprivations. But my bourgeois extraction did not impede me from preferring working-class people to that velvety, stagnant, bigoted simulation of class to which I belonged. For this I can thank my mother, who raised me with her submissive yet tenacious rebellion to that kind of "racism," which at the time was predominant and generic in the bourgeoisie and nobility. She taught me that "all the little girls and boys were the same as me" even if they didn't have nice clothes and toys and went to school only up to the third grade. Her origins as a wealthy mountain girl allowed me, during the long vacations at Monghidoro and the nearby towns, to have friends who were much more interesting than the "little lords" of the city. I became an expert at looking for blueberries, blackberries, mushrooms, and raspberries and good at climbing rocks and trees, familiar with inaccessible passages and rest stops on the mountain pastures from which I would return with my shepherd friends, dark from the sun and scratched by the thorns. In 1918, the war carried off two of our own family members and brought about the failure of our family business. I left my studies in the third year of classical high school, abandoning my dream of becoming a doctor, and, along with three of my dearest friends, I was forced to find a job immediately, to live. Among our circle of friends and rich relatives, in that mental emptiness, I found only vague offers of jobs as a children's governess, due to my culture and especially my knowledge of French, or as a companion to old people. These ambiguous situations were offered in either a charitable and paternalistic way, or more dangerously, as something to be manipulated in a kind of espionage on the other hired help. I was young, but proud and easily offended; I understood that I would be put up with in the first situation, and treated with suspicion in the other. In one clean break, I abandoned every rapport I had with the ranks of the bourgeoisie and left, first to be an orderly and then a nurse in hospitals. It was a job I liked because I had so wanted to study medicine. And even if it was a humble job, poorly paid and taxing, I never regretted it. And that's how I got my place in the working class.

Nineteen thirty-two was the year the Fascist regime decided to impose a party card on all government employees, dependents, and others, and problems and scandals followed. Whoever refused lost his job. Thus eleven tenured professors at the universities and heads of clinics, among them Professor Bartolo Nigrisoli, left their jobs. Only eleven names in all of Italy. The others preferred to continue on their merry way, deceiving themselves that they were conceding nothing to Fascism. Others, many others, belonged to the party with conviction. Maybe even Mussolini himself didn't believe he had such a following in the upper caste of the official intelligentsia. We at the hospital had to undergo a very hasty procedure: the director of each institute compiled the list of the personnel and made a request in alphabetical order. In the rite for obtaining the party card, there were to be two presenters, the director of the institute himself and someone else, chosen at random. Two signatures at the bottom of each list, and a salary deduction of ten lire "for the application." I was a nurse and got sixteen lire a day; the orderlies got exactly ten. One day of work, or almost, up in smoke, and what was worse, our names on those lists. They gave us receipts and we would have to go and get the card when a postcard arrived. The regime ran everything with postcards, from the call to arms to the imposition of participating in oceanic assemblies. In time, I received the postcard, but I didn't show up to get the card—not then, not ever.

In my condition as a girl alone—after the death of my mother, my father, and my nursemaid, the governess of thirty-five years of service in our family and who was the last to go—in a demanding job without a future, I lived in a temporary state, a state of detach-

ment, as if in an existence that wasn't my own. The go-
ings on of the country, of Fascism, of the government,
of the dictatorship, didn't really affect me. I was attached to the house, a small apartment bought with the
last remains of the bankruptcy. My rich furniture recon-
structed a picture of the past, silent and somewhat sad,
but in a certain way exciting. At the hospital I had become fond of the sick people, fond of my commitment,
not for a rhetorical sense of abnegation, but because
hard as it was, I liked it. I had many acquaintances with
whom I got along, but very few friends.

We did such long shifts that there was very little time
left for going out together, but when we did, it was to
the movies. In my ward for the chronically ill—a strange
quartering for emergencies that, like so many things in
our country, had gone on for ages—worked a blond
girl. She was a little chubby, and calm and sweet; her
name was Bianca Fontana. Although younger than I,
she was like an older sister, she was so good to me. I
went to her house often, and her mother made me
fried crescents, like my nanny used to for us children at
snack time. She had a beautiful peasant face, with light
blue eyes in a web of tight wrinkles at the corners when
she smiled. She told me how Bianca's brother and fiancé were working abroad, but no other details. Bianca
confided in me that she was embarrassed to answer
their letters, especially those of her fiancé. "I always
have to repeat the same things," she said. "I don't know
him by sight. We got engaged at a distance, by mail, because he's with my brother." It seemed to me quite a

strange thing, but I didn't want to be nosy. I came to know the truth the morning of the Fascist Party card. Bianca told me, crying, "My brother and fiancé are in prison, not working abroad," she said. "They must have done something," I thought stupidly, in my ignorance.

"Condemned by the special tribunal because they're Communists," Bianca said. "Now I can tell you; I trust you. But what can I do about this card? They won't give it to me because they'll investigate and find out that I'm related to a political prisoner. I'll lose my job."

It was a shock: in my protected life I didn't know that there were still political prisoners. It seemed to me the stuff of history books, something from the nineteenth century, Silvio Pellico, Spielberg* . . . But no, instead they were alive, present-day, and all because of those Blackshirts who anyway were always nasty to me, by instinct. I touched the ground as if I were getting off a hot-air balloon, and from that moment I hated all that was Fascist—their songs, their mottoes, their funereal aspect. I decided I would never get that card, and found a way so that Bianca was also spared that damage. Little by little she introduced me to other comrades, both male and female. I drafted my first notions of socialism, that fundamentally did not really differ that much from the naive teachings of my mother. All we could do was get together with other trusted people and talk, learn, and construct our hope and desire of a revolt—to begin, without realizing it, the Resistance.

* Silvio Pellico, Italian patriot and writer, was held in the Spielberg prison, an experience immortalized in his famous work *Le mie prigioni* (1832).

The first active gesture that I made was to go with Bianca on the road along the Reno Canal, along the outside wall of the Charter House, where the tomb of Zanardi's son had been marked in chalk. The day of the anniversary, we threw red carnations over the wall. Many people went in random order; there were long lines walking along the edge of the canal. One or two flowers remained on the top of the wall; they had flown high. Despite the two dark countenances who on the inside formed the armed guard, the morning after, the marble slab of Libero Zanardi was covered with red carnations.

For a pardon after five years of punishment, the political prisoners came home, even if in guarded freedom: Aurelio Fontana; Bianca's fiancé, whose name I forget; Mario Peloni, whose Elsa had been waiting for him for years; Maria Baroncini; and others. They came to my house the evening of their arrival, and we had a little party, dancing to the sound of a gramophone kept very low because of the neighbors. Bianca died of tuberculosis the twenty-first day of March 1935 and never came to know that in December I met, in a completely different set of circumstances, the comrade Antonio Meluschi, who had also been released from jail, where he had been with Aurelio, Mario, Leonildo Tarozzi, and others, and we married a few months later. He combed the disheveled tangle of my thoughts, and thus began my real schooling in the party. They were precarious days and years for us—full, radiant, fearful. We had visits from the police; the drafting of my husband, that twice resulted in nothing; the birth of our son,

Agostino. Little by little, toward the start of the war, they left us in peace. The Fascists had plenty to worry about. The ninth of September 1943, my companion left with Pino Beltrame and a clandestine radio transmitter. I helped the deserters of the destroyed army looking for civilian clothing, giving away all that remained of masculine apparel.

I began my partisan war in the company of fear. In the beginning, while I was still in Bologna, I was terrorized by the air raids. I couldn't imagine what the destruction of a house was like. I thought walls fell over like stage sets, invading all the spaces, creating mountains of walls one on top of the other, with people underneath, like strata of bodies covered on top by bricks, windows, doors, furniture. During the first bombings I saw, instead, that doorways, buildings, bell towers, fell apart; they were almost sucked into the void of the underground. Much less than I would have thought actually remained, and all of it was in pieces, dust, an unrecognizable pile where before there had been a building. You didn't see people very much; there were groups here and there along the pathways that were all that was left of the streets. But they appeared in haste, everyone going their own way, always anxiously running toward an unknown destination, or with strangely euphoric faces as if stupefied to still be alive.

For my own part, from the very first air-raid alarm, I had an aversion to the shelters. Uselessly, I repeated to myself that the dead were usually found outside, in the open. The ones who hadn't had time to take shelter, who had been caught by a displacement of air from an exploded bomb, that from a distance had thrown them against an intact wall. Many people, they told me, saved themselves simply by hiding in the basement. For me, that wait underground was impossible, in the terrible silence that followed the repeated scream of the alarm sirens. I held my breath to catch the drone of the planes, the unknown sounds of explosions that could have been those of the antiaircraft guns, but also maybe of the bombs. I hated like enemies the other people who were down there; by now, all of them were used to it, organized, experts. On top of it all, I would have liked to have slapped the ones who, without fail, furnished us with gratuitous information like "now they're over the train station, they're looking for the command posts and the barracks, they want to hit the airfield"; or the optimists who had friends and cousins in the air force and who assured us "Bologna is in such a position that from the air you can't see it." It often happened that I'd leave the shelter after trying my best to resist, but then I'd end up running out of there just as the bombing started, if there was a bombardment. I'd end up running toward the city gates, running on foot in that flood of motorcycles, cars, bikes, wagons, and sidecars that desperately rushed by. If anyone had fallen, it would have been a massacre. I was so afraid of what could happen to me that I started to find a kind of courage. The fact of the matter is that at that time I was alone, with my husband already a partisan and my child off in hiding, and so I got used to thinking that as long as I could see and hear, it meant I was alive. And so it was worth giving everything up and contenting oneself with just breathing. This was the secret of my every future force and my strength in the risky actions. It was useful even when I was back with my friends and family, in a moment that could have been fatal.

One fear alone I never forgot, and it was retrospective. I experienced it without knowing it and only realized it the next day. Even now, if it happens that I can't sleep and the memory of that moment comes to mind, I feel the same chill, maybe the most unpleasant and intense one of my entire life. It happened when we were in the Campotto Valley, an immense basin between the roads, in the environs of Argenta. It is a low-lying land that in summer is full of cane and swamp grass and in winter fills with water and mud. There's a collection drain that runs through it and, by means of a dike, it helps clear a vast territory of fields and orchards that would otherwise be covered by the overflow from the banks of the Reno, even during the first rains. We went there at the beginning of August 1944, when the partisans were still dragging forward the so-called advance of the Allies in Tuscany. We thought that Alexander,* knowing he could rely on us, would have attacked the Gothic line and liberated Northern Italy. We were ready, entire brigades of us, to pave the way. And then he would have had the help of the cities that

* Famous British General Sir Harold Alexander, a key commander in the Allied efforts in Italy. Recent scholarship finds Alexander's ability to lead was "overrated" (see D'Este, *Bitter Victory*, 334ff.)

little by little would have rebelled. Instead, he got to Florence after everything had already been done, and he slowed everything down until the April of the following year. We didn't know it, however, or we never would have chosen that spot. Campotto was for summers, for building cane huts, for digging out antifire trenches and to pile up provisions that would have been used for the population in the dangerous moment of the "passage of the front." We spoke like that, with ingenuity, about "the passage of the front," as if it were a fleeting and rapid eventuality, while quite on the contrary, the front stopped after they took Ravenna. They readied the winter lodgings whose tormented trajectory ran into Alfonsine, a few kilometers away. Alexander made his proclamation that everyone could go home until springtime.

In the meantime, during those scorching August days we had a detachment of partisans in Campotto, and we lived among the yellow canes that didn't make one thread of shade. It seemed like we were in an African landscape, and we became dark as Bedouins. My husband was busy elsewhere and I had the task of feeding everyone (helped only by one woman and two men), of keeping an eye on the place, of responding to the strangers who came along the paths looking for purple willow. I would tell these people that we were camped out down there for fear of the hammering bombardments that hit the roads and the bridge of the Bastia River, at San Biagio on the Reno. I had my son, who was not quite seven years old, with me, and even in the life of a partisan brigade, I never wanted to be sepa-

rated from him. In fact, in that strange sojourn, he had
a ball. The "boys" spoiled him to death, and during nap
time, they made him little carts of toothpicks and little
brooms with the tufts of cane. Then they disappeared at
night, going into battle on the roads, hunting the
German transports that they often turned upside down,
wheels in the air in the moonlight, and then the Anglo-
American bombers called "Pippo" would pass by, to
take credit for dropping bombs on the fires.

In the morning they came back along the path of the
Traversante, reaching the camp, and then they disappeared, quietly and barefoot among the rustling stalks
of cane. All they needed was to stretch out in that warm,
yellow reverberation a few steps away, and they were invisible. They slept like logs with their heads shaded by a
leafy branch and their whole bodies in the sun. At noon
we brought them things to eat, one at a time, if we
thought there might be some "purple willow" woman
nearby, or we got together in that spot that served as
the "village square." This was actually a clearing where
the canes had all been cut down to make a space to
light a fire. We had to be extremely careful because it
was fire season and the entire dry basin could have
spontaneously, suddenly blazed, and that would have
been a fine mess. I must say, I didn't even think of it at
the time.

My son Agostino, called "Bu," had become perfectly
integrated, and he moved about with the fragile gait of
a small valley animal, without a voice, in the midst of
"those boys." That's how he referred to them, and even
after, up to the Liberation that became a magic word

for us, for him and me, like *les maitres-mots* of Mowgli's animals in Kipling's *Jungle Book*. "Those boys" meant something to us, something very private and about which we could make no mention to anyone else. And never did he, small as he was, give the secret away. Even now, it happens that we refer to "those boys," and this for us means "the partisans."

This unusual vacation was brusquely interrupted because of two imbeciles who certainly were not partisans, but they did go ahead and shoot two unarmed Germans who had gone fishing. One was killed and the other wounded. This happened right at the mouth of the Traversante, involving the valley where the camp stood in the retaliation. Already that very same evening we saw flames rising up in the distance, near the town of Campotto. At dawn, the partisans advised us to save ourselves because they were going with their weapons to other territories. "Escape right away!" they told us. "The Germans will burn the valley."

The woman who was helping me, one of the many Agneses, was afraid and wanted to leave right away, but I thought of the supplies, of the tools, of the kitchen utensils, the necessary things we had down there. And I decided, incautiously, to stay, to hide at least the most important things. The two men were persuaded only with great effort, and we started to transport the stuff to the riverbank. We loaded a boat that had been abandoned in a canal, filling it with supplies, since it was tied at the shore among the bulrush, the high grass, and the mire. It was stiflingly hot and after many heavy trips back and forth, night fell. We were dazed and in a stupor with fatigue. Who knows why, maybe it was one of my crazy ideas, strangely sure as I was of that refuge among the canes, we waited for it to get dark. And then we embarked on the walk home, and we reached the dike. Deserted: the guards had left.

There was a construction that bridged the turbid and swift waters of the collector drain. There was no road to cross, only some sort of balcony around the house, not wider than a meter, and encircled by a railing. Or so it seemed to us in the uncertain light of the moon that had not yet risen. But the railing was interrupted every so often by an empty space, from which the shutters were operated. We ventured out in a line on this passageway in the clamor of the dark torrent that passed below. I was so tired I didn't think to take the child's hand, and he went in front of me brushing along the wall without touching the railing. And luckily no one moved toward that railing that was missing in spots, otherwise one step would have been enough to plunge into the current. One misstep would have been enough to fall into the darkness, especially the child who sleepily groped along. One step, one splash, and his little black shadow would have disappeared; and I would have followed him instinctively, with no hope but that of dying quickly, the two of us.

Instead, we realized nothing; we reached the riverbank and breathed the tender freshness of a field. We slept a little later on, behind a shed where the current of the canal ended up in the river in a delicious rustle of calm water. But we were awakened by Germans who were shooting from the riverbank into the valley with ri-

fles and tracer bullets. During the night they sent soldiers with flamethrowers to destroy the huts of our "village" in long stripes of flame. And in half an hour, the
basin of dry cane became a bonfire.

A few days later, hardheaded as I am, I returned to
the place to assure myself that nothing else needed to
be salvaged. I crossed the dike and saw in the light of
day the tight passage and the empty places where the
railing was missing over the roaring torrent above the
canal, the green water, dense with algae, three meters
deep. It was then that I suffered that attack of retrospective fear from which I have not yet completely recovered.

Of this episode I want to remember the woman who
followed me, terrified, but without hesitation. She was a
unique "Agnese," different from all the others. Who
knows what incidents brought her at a very young age
to prostitution. She had lived for years in brothels,
changing cities every "fortnight or so" and not knowing
anything of those cities but the street from the train station to the "place of work," as if they were all alike.

One day a man from the countryside fell in love with
her and took her out of that life, making her his wife.
She, too, had a kind of retrospective fear, as if she were
living a dream from which she might wake up. She told
me about so many grim and shameful things with perfect innocence, as if they hadn't happened to her.
Except for some license in her language, which did not
appear coarse, but rather like a memory, an echo almost, like someone who has lived for a long time in a

foreign country. Now she was a housewife, ambitious about her new furniture. She had transported to that savage valley a shining credenza, and she was very upset she hadn't managed to finish it with a glass window to show off her stemware. We found our stuff in the boat, but the Germans had thrown a hand grenade inside. The boat had sunk into the mud, a pile of scraps. "Too bad for the flour and the pasta," I said. And she answered, "You can't have everything." But I realized she was crying in the silence, maybe for her credenza.

As much as I think about it, I cannot remember this woman's name. It began with *A:* Adele or Amalia. I know she had to leave the town later, where her husband was derided by everyone because he had gotten his wife from a whorehouse. I'm sorry to have lost touch with her and to have forgotten her name. But I hope she's living in peace like the other real housewives, and that she's been able to buy all the furniture she wanted, that she liked so much.

Once, when we were already close to the springtime offensive, the Anglo-American bombers began seminating the terrain for the advance. We saw a reconnaissance plane pass over our plain between Alfonsine and Argenta. We had the command in the Rustica Malveduta, a house of stones and mud that seemed to remain standing only miraculously. More precisely, our address was the Visentini House, which was another cottage less than one hundred meters from the barn, now empty of livestock and bursting with families that had escaped the incendiary bombs that seemed to bull's-eye the most random structures.

My husband, the commander of the area, had had the inhabitants of Mulino di Filo construct two kinds of shelters because of the insufficient cover. In that swampy drainage land, you found water at a depth of one and a half meters, as if it were a large sponge. These constructions, however, were reinforced and spacious enough, and covered with crossed beams and wood from railroad ties taken from the railroad bridge that had been destroyed in heavy air raids that would have been enough to level half a city. The Allied aviators did great things, but willing or not, they had bad aim! Anyway, that time the reconnaissance plane thought it saw who knows what military objective in the pile of houses at Mulino di Filo, and it emitted a kind of white smoke. Immediately, we heard the musical sound of motors in formation, and the sound of bombs falling near and far, a roar, a trembling of the earth that seemed to fill the entire horizon. "Inside, inside!" and down went the women and screaming children into the modest shelter; with the stomping of feet they began to sweat humidly. Naturally, I was outside; I had a horror as usual of closed places. I felt less than ever like staying still under the railroad ties, with the thought of all that could have happened if a bomb fell on top of us. "Go down," my new husband and commander said, who in certain moments treated me as if I were the last of the rookies. "Absolutely not," I responded.

I ran to the other shelter, where there was some confusion because of a woman who had fainted, and in the meantime the explosions had become a wall of sound. I saw beyond the Fossetta a little, dry stream bed that separated the threshing grounds from the fields. A man was running along the path, his arms open wide, and he was shouting "Help! Help!" Suddenly in front of me I found Armando Montanari, called E'Desch, who told me about a disaster that had happened a short distance away, beyond the road to town. Even my husband called me, saying, "Take the bags," and he got on a bicycle, putting one of the bags on the handlebars. I took the other and got on E'Desch's handle bars; he was already leaving. The shopping bags were all we had in the way of medicine, injections, and first aid materials that were more or less efficient. We had gathered the supply during months and months of lies, of old prescriptions, of purchases in honest pharmacies that needed to get rid of stock that was in danger of going bad, or even on the black market from professionals who were not so scrupulous. In those days it was a treasure for which I felt responsible as the keeper, because this was a zone without doctors. And if nothing else, I had had a long experience as a nurse in a hospital.

Unfortunately I didn't know how to ride a bike, a rather inconvenient handicap in that expanse of plains. But I had won a kind of championship for riding on handlebars, which meant you had to let yourself go like a dead weight because everyone transported bags and bundles that way, and it was a normal means of transport. You just had to rest the outside of the right thigh, holding onto the bar with one hand, and stretch out your feet together so as not to get stuck in the pedals. The driver zipped along as if he were all alone. If you became stiff or clutched on, or if you trembled, it meant you would skid and fall. I, so small and light and in control of my nerves, did not constitute a problem, and I almost always managed to strike such a balance with my "driver" that it allowed us to go down the sinuous paths of the riverbanks, to go over the bumps between roads and fields, to ride along over underbrush without getting off. Even this time it was like this, but all of a sudden, "E'Desch" brusquely swerved off the path, shouting back to my husband who was following us hot on our heels. "Hurry, hurry!" I didn't have a chance with my myopic eyes to glimpse the thread of white-gray smoke that we had already passed, but I understood after an angry explosion of something that expanded in the air like a gust of wind. "Have no fear," said the voice of my companion and commander, always too dangerously optimistic in my opinion. "An unexploded fragmentation bomb!" We had avoided it by a hair's breadth and it had exploded behind us. It was one of those bombs from the fighter-bombers that needed to be handled in a strange way because they made a huge rose of big and small fragments, and the smallest of these that touched the skin would surely produce an infection. There were those who said the infection was due to an old infestation of malaria that had existed years before in these low-lying lands. But they were unchecked rumors, because lots of other people that happened to be down there from regions where the fine air had never hosted malaria found themselves with the same deep, exuding penetrations that became pus. The same old mysteries of prohibitive scientific experiments applied to the actions of a merciless war!

We crossed the street that divided the village and also marked the border between the provinces of Ferrara and Ravenna. The so-called Allies had warned with their usual little leaflets—"Italy at war"—dropped by the planes that the bombings would be executed two hundred meters from the route of the streets, avoiding the groups of houses that flanked them. But as usual, the pilots suffered from inexactitude in their aim, or lack of practice, or they didn't keep their promise; a good way short of the two hundred meters, we found ourselves in front of frightful holes and piles of rubble. Screams of the wounded, cries of the survivors, dusty immobility of the dead. We worked hard around the mangled bodies, freeing them from the stones and broken furniture. We saw dead children with their little faces still shining from tears and life. It seemed impossible that they would never again get up and run in their broken shoes. I remember a woman with her flesh so torn up with open wounds that it was difficult to find a strip of flesh intact enough to give her a tetanus shot. And I remember a beautiful girl with blond curls whose breast had been ripped apart by a fragment of iron; she was like some kind of stupendous, mutilated statue. Yet they both were saved. I saw them again, healed, after many months. The first was able to get back use of her legs and arms; the younger one was still beautiful, like an Amazon, with only one breast. I had not forgotten their faces; but they, naturally, returned from the edge of death, did not recognize me.

Tired of seeing blood and lives destroyed, we went back along the street to our house. This time it was not easy to keep myself steady on the bars, and even my vigorous E'Desch had to struggle to hold up that sack of potatoes that I had become against his arm. And right against the wall of the Rustica Malveduta we found a German—all the others from the house were in the shelter or busy in action—and he had been keeping an eye on Judith, Armando's mother, who was a little old lady with hardly any breath left in her due to a heart condition. But she was afraid of nothing. He was black from the earth, as he had nearly been involved in an explosion, but he didn't seem wounded. He had a dirty sweater and a jacket that was torn to shreds, but you could see on the lapels of his shirt collar the little serpentine strips of the SS. In that moment I scarcely felt the solidarity imposed by my profession, and I would have gladly left him there to whimper hoarsely against that wall.

But the imperious nod of my husband was not lacking, always in control of himself, and I undid the shopping bags. I made the man lie down, examined him and medicated the few, light contusions. Then I indicated he should wash himself in a bucket from the well and I went in behind Judith to drink something to get the dust out of my throat. It was just a second, but when I came back out to get the "pharmacy," the damned Nazi had already left with my shopping bags. We looked for him everywhere, along the Fossetta, among the canes of the swamp—but who knows how, he'd been quite quick. We didn't find him, not then, not later.

Maybe he'd met one of his own men, or had some means of getting away, a motorscooter or a bike. The fact is that I no longer had anything of my medicines, not a precious box of shots, nor an even more precious but skimpy supply of tetanus shots. Nothing. And with the "passage of the front" imminent, and the usual preparation of carpet-bombing! I swore that never again, in spite of the international laws, would I extend a hand to cure an enemy—an enemy like that one, an SS.

Easter in the year 1945 fell on April 1, and it was no April Fools'. We all knew that the next day, the long-awaited spring offensive would finally begin on the part of the Allies, almost a year late—the so-called Liberation. For us partisans it meant clearing the terrain of the remaining Germans, from the first to the last; otherwise the Anglo-Americans would not have made even the smallest step forward. The Allies had been behind the lines for six months on the Alfonsine front and were now intent on throwing grenades like no tomorrow. Many of them were aimed at villages and many more were wasted on the marshy deserts and on the liquid expanse of the valley. Our task was no small undertaking, because the Nazis on their own showed themselves to be rather difficult to move (the Black Brigade Fascists had already disbanded some time ago, and in various ways had disappeared). It was even necessary that the partisans take the trouble to let the Allied command know, "Forward! Come! Here, there's no one left!"

The Sunday of the Olive Tree, as it was called, we were all very busy. Our commander left at dawn for a meeting in the open countryside where representatives of the parties were to meet to constitute a new CLN. Already three or four such organisms, difficult yet necessary to the functioning of the war, had been destroyed by betrayals and ambushes, and their officials shot, assassinated, or gone missing in the German camps.

I had been given the task, along with Terzilla Montanari, the most combative of my Agneses, of fetching a certain little suitcase that contained the stamps and documents of the Mario Babini Brigade (the formation of the Valleys of Comacchio, Campotto, and Argenta). This would become indispensable for proving our conduct to the Allies. This little suitcase was hidden in a hole in a wall of a country house a few kilometers away, that up to a few months earlier had been the command's headquarters. We had abandoned it under the pressure of the Goering Division come from Norway to renew with fresh energy the by-now bloodless troops that had been holding the front. We had to hide, therefore, the most important things and continually change the men in the so-called barracks that were really nothing but peasant houses from the reclaimed land. This area had become a valley after the Germans had mined the riverbanks and opened the dikes to slow down the invasion.

Terzilla pulled the corners of the black kerchief she wore on her head under her chin, a real Agnese gesture, and we headed off across the fields. The house we had lived in that horrible winter, so cold and dangerous, was in the small village of Menate. There we had found little collaboration and downright hostility on the part of the inhabitants. They were strange people, very different from those at Mulino di Filo, fearful and greedy. They had attached themselves to the Germans who were occupying the town. It was a subsistence company, pretty well supplied, that was trying to keep in the people's good graces in order to live in peace, and in their free time even have fun with the girls. It so happened that we had to stop there because there was a pretty wide canal that allowed us to reach the boats of the Comacchio rowers from inland. These boats were indispensable for the refurnishing of supplies to our companies in the middle of that mirror of water in the valley. But we had to put up with the people of Menate and scare them more than the Germans did to be able to maintain our lucky system.

When we finally arrived home, we found a cold and unfriendly welcome. Only the farmer Michele was persuaded by the necessity to take action. I like to remember him as understanding; he died later, during the last bombings. But his women, his wife and daughters, when they learned why we had gone, became furious. It needs to be said that in those days it was common practice to wall up the most valuable things, to bury bicycles, sewing machines, linens, and even alarm clocks to protect oneself from the German raids. But for us who knew the precise location of the hiding place, it was only a question of ripping a piece of plaster off the wall, getting out the suitcase, and then giving it one more wipe of cement. It was a job that took at most half an hour in a little room where the Germans never went. But instead, other women came forward. They, too, had their things hidden in this wall. They threatened me, they blocked me in a corner of the kitchen shouting that we were thieves, that we wanted to take everything. Michele took his wife in his arms as she was about to become hysterical and he dragged her outside. In the meantime, Terzilla had disappeared and it looked bad for me. A German marshall who lived upstairs passed by and the girls called him, screaming like hyenas. But the German didn't want to have anything to do with civilians' problems, and he called two soldiers from the courtyard and went upstairs without answering. And right in that moment, Terzilla, with her beautiful lean Etruscan face and with a small hatchet in her hand, said in dialect, "Anyway, I've already made a hole in the wall." Pandemonium broke out! They beat us, and I had to find a remedy for a black eye. They wanted to throw us in the canal, but we already had the suitcase and just outside the first camp we met Armando, E'Desch, and Cencio, who had realized how late we were and had come to look for us with a P38 under his overalls.

And forward with the advance! The bulletins from Radio London, Ta ta ta ta, Ta ta ta ta—hammering the first solemn notes of Beethoven's Fifth, gave us astounding news: "The Anglo-American Army advances and is on the right bank of the Menate River." That is to say, that canal where the fast boats of Comacchio, a meter wide and eight meters long, had to enter with the prow straight and the stern behind, otherwise they couldn't turn around. Or "Formations of fighter-bombers demolish the positions at Mulino di Filo." This was clear, bombs were falling like rain. But the "positions" were all the isolated houses on the plain; and in the meantime, the Germans, driven out by the partisans, were scattering in the ditches, in the little manholes, and they were sniping on the towpaths of the old riverbanks.

The eleventh day under the fragmentation bombs, the fourth child of Albina was born. She had been widowed a few months earlier, and this child would never know his father. I had to be the midwife, and in that occasion I was afraid not so much of the explosions as I was that either mother or child would perish of some complication. Instead, a nine-pound baby boy arrived with the so-called benediction of the "madonna's shirt" or rather a white and slimy skin on the little body. In the scarce religious faith of those places, it had no effect on anyone. Near me was the most quiet and most courageous of my Agneses, Maria Margotti, always the first to help. She was also the first to show up in '49 on the banks of the Dead Sea, leaving this life under the fire of a dry, hard, leaden rifle that resembled her own machine-gun.

And forward to the Liberation! The first English I saw were huddled against an embankment and were shooting toward the walls of the brickworks. A German tank parked behind the corner of the Bragagliolo house was raging with the cannons, and one of the English made an angry gesture at me to order me to throw myself on the ground. There wasn't a living soul around. Only the rumbles and explosions, the rolling of the rifles, and the whistle of the fighter planes nose-diving.

I was going, incidentally, to look for help for the partisan Fabio, caught by the sniper fire of a damned Nazi; a wound gaped in the upper thigh, with the bullet lodged inside. Now he was going to die of internal bleeding on a bed frame stripped of its mattress in the barn of the Visentini house. And he knew he was dying. "It was useless coming here with so much danger," he said to me, "and don't you go looking for anyone." In our last day of the war, one of the last shots of the enemy had gotten him—he, who had been a soldier since 1940, first in the regular army and then as a guerrilla in Yugoslavia and Italy, five years of fighting without so much as a scratch.

I knew that at the Petronici house a section of the English medical services had arrived and set up a field hospital. I deluded myself into thinking that by arriving in time, Fabio could be saved by an emergency operation. They said the seriously wounded were unloaded and taken in the back. Instead, when I got to Petronici's, they were unloading their own, English and Scottish, with weapons and baggage and bagpipes. And that meant the Germans had made a ferocious about-face; the entire zone was iron and fire, and we were trapped in the middle with the civilian population.

It was a never-ending day, with death continually at our side. A twelfth of April as dark as November, with low clouds from which no rain fell and no fog, but almost a scattered wind, drenched and chilling. I had lost contact with my loved ones. The commander with his men had certainly run to find out where the attacks were coming from, from that one, solitary tank, so that the Allies would be able to hit it squarely without sustaining damage themselves. I had left even my own child with the women of Pecorara, a house of peasants in which more than four hundred civilians were amassed, removed from the street, but not so much so that a bomb couldn't fall on it, certainly. It seemed to me that nothing too bad should happen in a day like that. I was aware of the great superiority of the partisan army over the regular troops. That is, in the latter, an action is ordered if you have rank, while the partisans got their rank from the efficacy of the action. "We can't make a mistake," I thought, "right at the last moment."

This was the war in our valley that is neither sea nor river nor lake, but stagnant, white water, tossed between hills and dales when there is wind, more muddy and soggy than the sky, filled with algae, with underwater currents, threatening roads of water, recognizable only in the chiaroscuro of the surface and in the instinct of those who are born and raised here and who learn how to swim and drive boats before they put their feet on firm ground. These were the places and landscapes of my life that I often believed I was seeing for the last time. Maybe I have spoken too much of myself, but what I am proud of is "my" war, the one against fear. Because I was denied the encounter, the happiness, the relief, the ardor of Victory. I did not see exultant crowds, nor hugs, nor flags in the sun.

I felt safe and sound in a horizon of rain, among shots and explosions, on the front. And that was, for me, the day of Liberation.

About the Author

Renata Viganò was the author of several books of poetry, fiction, and nonfiction. She is best known for her novel *L'Agnese va a morire*, which was adapted for cinema by Giuliano Montaldo in the 1970s.

About the Translator

Suzanne Branciforte is a member of the Foreign Languages Department at the University of Genoa in Italy. She is the author of *Parliamo italiano!*